LITTLE Bear
Becoming a Brave

DANIEL PHELPS

ISBN
978-1-956529-38-8 (Paperback)
978-1-956529-37-1 (eBook)

Table of Contents

Chapter One 1

Chapter Two 5

Chapter Three...11

Chapter Four..15

Chapter Five...21

Chapter Six 27

Chapter Seven 33

Chapter Eight 37

Chapter Nine 43

Chapter Ten 49

Chapter Eleven...53

Chapter Twelve 59

Chapter Thirteen...65

Chapter Fourteen 71

Chapter Fifteen...77

Chapter Sixteen 85

Chapter Seventeen...89

Chapter Eighteen 95

Chapter Nineteen..101

Chapter Twenty...107

Chapter Twenty One...111

Chapter Twenty Two 117

Chapter Twenty Three 123

Chapter Twenty Four 131

Chapter Twenty Five 137

Chapter Twenty Six...143

Chapter
ONE

Little Bear was on his own; for the first time. He had reached the age, and maturity to prove himself. He had watched his father, and listened to his instructions of how to hunt, and live off of the land. He knew he was ready. He knew he could survive, and prove his manhood to the tribe. And he wanted, so bad, to get a better name than Little Bear.

He need to live, in the forest, from this moon to the next moon, alone. He needed to perform an act to show his ability as a brave. He would show his father that he was a man. And he would impress wild flower. He intended to have her as his woman. He planned to be a heralded member of the tribe. He would be as admired as Bear slayer, or buffalo hunter, who showed great strength, and hunting prowess. He would have stories to tell to the tribe.

But, for now he was alone. He would be very cautious. There were bears and wild cats in the forest, and buffalo in the meadows. His life depended on how well he listened, and what he saw. Every sound tells a story, his father had told him. The difference between a leaf crackling, and a twig snapping could be the difference in eating rabbit, or deer, or it could also be the difference between life and death.

By the time the sun was high in the sky, Little Bear had past all of the places he had known in his youth. He could not be found along the trails the tribe traveled. Little Bear was determined to become a man. He walked for a while longer and came to a stream. He would spend his first night here.

There would be fish, and berries, he would eat well, and sleep well. Everything was going very well this day. There was plenty of wood for a fire, and twigs and dry leaves.

Little Bear was cutting the fifth mark on his spear. Five days and nothing worth talking about happened. But it had been a wonderful time. His communion with nature, the birds, the trees, the lakes and streams served him well. And he had been thankful for all the spirits were giving him. It was time too look for a place to camp. He could smell water nearby, and had seen the animals heading toward the water.

There was a new sound. It was not the usual animals he had been hearing. He smelled the air, because the sound came from upwind. He noticed a different odor. This was a herd, or group of some kind. Too loud for smaller animals. Perhaps the buffalo were coming. The herd was getting nearer so Little Bear found a tree to climb into to watch them go by. It was then he heard human voices. He could not understand these sounds. But, he understood the tone. Some commanding, some answering the commands, some complaining, he understood the tones. But not the words. Little Bear watched as men, and horses and wagons flowed into the meadow by the lake.

"Set up camp Sergeant"

"Yes sir"

Little Bear had never seen people like his before. The clothes they wore, the wagons were all beyond anything Little Bear had ever seen. He watched as wagons were unloaded, and tents began to grow.

There were more people here than he had ever seen, even at the meetings of the tribes. He thought about joining their camp, but, decided it would be better to wait and see what kind of people these were. His father told him not all people were good people. He had heard of the wars between the tribes.

That some tribes took from other tribes, and would kill. He didn't see any arrows, or bows, or even a spear anywhere.

He watched as the wagons with women and children were encircled by the men in the strangle clothes. The women went to the water and children began to play. Some ran to the water and splashed around. It must be some tribe he had never heard of. Their fathers had not taught them well about nature, he thought. It will be hard to fish will all of that noise and moving the water so much.

It was some time before Little Bear heard the loud sound from the big sticks the men carried.

It scared Little Bear. He watched the fire come out of the stick. And he saw the men bring in a deer for their supper. He had never heard a story like this before. He wanted to know more.

He noticed that these people did not seem very friendly, even to each other. Some were laughing and playing, some were yelling and angry, and some were quiet, but all listened to the ones who were, apparently, in charge. Little Bear remained very still, and very quiet until he was pretty sure all were asleep. He took notice that there were still several men walking around the camp. He slowly climbed down from his perch to inspect this new tribe. He crept into the camp watching and listening to hear if anyone came near. There was still food left around. That bothered him a lot. He knew food left out would draw the animals to feed. He tasted a piece of meat.

"This tasted different "he thought, "How does deer taste different than it did when the tribe cooked it?" And he liked it.

Little Bear heard the footsteps and crept back into the bushes. One of the walkers passed by.

After he was sure the man was gone he crept back and took enough meat to fill himself for the night.

Now he had a story to tell, but, it wasn't over yet. He wanted to learn more about this new tribe.

He had never heard of men with hair on their face. And these people were so pale.

He tried to remember if any stories of fire sticks had been told, but could think of none. They did not act like the people he knew. They did not dress like the people he knew. They did not talk like people he knew. Their clothes were not of skins, (at least not the skins he knew of).

Little Bear was tired. It had been a long day. He would sleep now. He told himself to sleep lightly. He must be able to get away if there was any trouble. He must take his time and learn enough to know if these were good, or bad people.

"Only the foolish rush in to trouble. "He remembered his father saying, "Be sure you know if you are running into a meadow or a swamp."

Chapter
TWO

Little Bear awoke to the strange noises of the new tribe. He took his place in the tree to watch how this people lived. He had seen so many things that he had been taught not to do. Just the fact that these people did not seem to care how much noise they made. They did not care that the animals were scared away. They did not seem to care what effect they were having on the natural neighborhood.

They were trampling down the herbs and flowers all around the area. He noticed many tools he had not seen before. Like the women at the lake with wooden boards rubbing their clothes and making a strange foam that drifted into the lake.

Little Bear decided to try to understand the words they were using. He listened to them talk.

"How long do you think we'll be staying here?"

This was a question, little Bear thought.

"Just for today, Just enough time for the scouts to locate our next stop."

"It has been three weeks since we left the fort. How much longer must we go before we decide to settle?"

"Well, we've crossed the gap, and we're in unknown territory. I would assume we will be building a town as soon as we find an area we can secure and defend."

Little Bear studied the words. We left the fort, we go before we decide, we've crossed, we will, we find, we can. That we word kept coming up. And the questions seemed to begin with how.

"Momma, see the way I made a fort with rocks/"

"Yes, dear, come and eat your breakfast now."

Little Bear realized this was a mother and child. Momma, had to be the mother, Yes, Dear would be the child's name. Yes Dear followed Momma around the tent to where the food was.

"Corporal!"

A man came running and put his hand up to his brow and said, "Yes, Sergeant!"

"The captain wants our platoon to secure this area. We can't take any chances that we might be attacked from any direction. See to it. Get some guards out here!"

"Yes Sergeant!"

So, yes sergeant was a chief, and corporal was a brave. And more we words. Little Bear was not sure what he was hearing, but hoped it would make sense soon.

Suddenly there was the sound of a fire stick in the distance. The whole camp changed the women grabbed the children and brought them into the wagons. The men grabbed their fire sticks and took up positions around the camp. Two men came running out of the forest and yelled at the men.

"We're under attack! Injuns are coming!"

It wasn't long before the fire sticks began making noise on the west side of the camp. Little Bear heard the yells of a rival tribe attacking the camp. He recognized the colors of the renegade tribe that had raided his tribe many times. The fire sticks were knocking them down easily, and they weren't getting back up. Those fire sticks were killing many braves. He watched as the arrows and spears flew into the camp and some found their targets, but they were no match for the fire sticks.

The battle was over in minutes. The renegades would not risk any more men from a direct assault, but the war was not over. The renegades would try to find places to attack around the camp.

Like a swarm of bees, once you disturb their colony, they will sting until they are dead. A spear would fly, and a scream would follow, then the fire sticks would answer.

Little Bear was secure in his tree. He was sure he could not be seen, unless he moved. He looked around and a saw a brave creeping underneath his tree. He was getting very close to the wagon where Yes Dear, and Momma were. There were no men near by. Little Bear did not want the mother and child to be hurt. He dropped from his hiding place, and ran toward the intruder. The brave flung open the cloth that covered the opening and raised his knife to stab the occupants. Little Bear was fast and struck first with his knife. He stood for a moment. He had never killed a man before. Momma and Yes Dear started at Little Bear. He started back, for just a minute, and then ran back into the forest.

What would he do now. Momma and Yes dear both knew he was there. They would look for him now. Panic set in. He thought to run, but remembered there were enemy tribesmen out there. He decided that no one had found his hiding place yet. He would stay hidden. Little Bear could feel his chest pounding. A fear he had never felt before. Stuck between two forces they may both want him dead. It will be a great story, if he gets back home to tell it.

There were screams coming from the wagon, and men ran to the wagon.

"That indian was going to kill us!" Momma cried, "A young indian killed him first."

"Which way did he go ma'am?" The corporal asked, "We'll get him for you."

"He saved our lives, Momma answered, "And he looked more scared than we were. He ran away and as long as he didn't kill us too, let him go."

"But ma'am," The corporal pleaded, "Just because he ran away doesn't mean he wont come back and kill you later, that's the way some red skins are."

Momma's tone became very angry. "Look soldier, that boy had more than enough time to get to us before you even knew either of them were around. And I saw the look on his face. He is just a kid, and he was saving us not attacking us. I will not send you out to kill a kid that saved me and my son's life!"

Turning from the woman, the corporal sent out a few men to search the area, realizing he was wasting his time arguing with the lady. Little Bear did not move a muscle as the scout searched through the area. There were some commotion where the searchers had gone. Little Bear heard a fire stick sound, then another, Momma started to cry. Two of the searchers returned hauling a third searcher between them.

"We found four or five of them injuns holed up out there." One offered, "Glad we got em, that may have been the rest of the war party corporal."

"You didn't see any more out there?"

"No, looked like that group were setting in for the night, or somethin, and there weren't no more."

"Any of em look like a kid?" The corporal asked.

Momma's head lifted as she listened.

"No, corporal, these were all growed men." The searcher answered.

Momma sighed and smiled lightly.

"What happened to private Martin?"

"Got stabbed before we could get em all, corporal, "the searcher answered, "Ain't too bad though, should be good in a few days."

The wounded man spoke up, "I gets me a life threatnin wound and you talkin bout just a few days, let me cut your side open, see how quick you get over it Bixby."

There was laughter, and then the corporal commanded, "Get that man to the doc's wagon before he bleeds to death!"

Little Bear watched as the tension subsided and the men separated and went their separate ways.

But one man remained in that area, walking back and forth, keeping and eye out for other attackers. He still had not been seen. And he was very happy he had not run any further back into the forest. And, he began to realize he had not eaten yet today. Not much hope of hunting for food now. And the berries were not where he could collect them without one of the men with fire sticks seeing him. And water was on the other side of the camp. But, he was still alive, and still hidden from those unknown people.

Chapter

THREE

As the sun got lower in the sky Little Bear could smell the food cooking. From time to time the wind blew the smell in his direction. He was hungry, but, he could think of no way to get anything to eat. He was still focused on trying to figure out this new tribe.

He watched as Momma came around the wagon. She looked to see where the man was who was walking back and forth, and came toward the forest. She had something in her hand. She went under the tree, to the other side. She looked around and said, "If you are still here, my angel, I have some warm food for you." She put the thing down and walked back to the wagon.

Little Bear wasn't sure what to do, but that thing she had put there smelled pretty good. He crept down from his perch, after waiting to see if anyone was coming to watch. Once he tasted the food, it didn't take him long to finish it off. He felt much better, and now he felt he had made a friend.

The sun was almost gone when Momma came back to the thing she lad left the food in. She picked it up and looked around.

"Well, I guess you were hungry, didn't leave a drop." She chided, "Mine is the best stew you'll find this side of colonies. We'll see how you like oatmeal in the morning. Have a pleasant evening angel boy."

She was using the same tone she had used with Yes Dear, Little Bear thought. She must like him. He watched her walk back to the wagon.

"What are you doing out here! The walker demanded, "Don't you know there could be more injuns out there?"

"I am sure there are, private." Momma Answered, "I am sure there are."

Ma'am, it's my job to keep you safe," The private complained, "I can't do that if you go wanderin off now, can I?"

"I'll take it from here, private!" the newcomer commanded, "Get back to your patrol."

"Yes sir, Major!" The private answered and walked away.

"Why are you making our job harder, Audrey?" The Major asked.

"There's a young boy out there that's hungry. He kept me and your son from getting killed today."

Momma replied.

"Yes, I heard there was trouble over here," The Major admitted, as he put his arms around Momma.

"I wish I'd known in time to come and help out. I was worried about you."

Momma kissed the Major and said, "And I was worried about you. I heard several men were hurt in the battle today. What Happened?"

"Yeah, I wondered how things would go with Chadwick and Morris doing the scouting." The Major began, "Seems they ran into some local tribe and had to start trouble. Those two are about as sneaky as a hungry ox. There ain't no injuns fer miles they said. Came runnin back all cut and bruised."

"Why did you send them out if they are that bad?" Momma asked.

I didn't." The Major replied, "The colonel picked them, said they were to take the duty. He was punishing them for something they did, and, he wanted to get them out of his sight for a while."

Little Bear watched as the Major's eyes began to look up into the trees. He froze for a moment when it looked like the Major was looking right at him, but the Major made no indication that he saw him.

"You say this was a boy?" the Major prodded, "an indian boy?"

"He couldn't have been more than 13 or 14 years old." Momma answered, "I think he was more afraid of us than he was of the indian he killed. I wonder why he decided to defend us? I saw the look on his face when he realized what he had done. He turned awfully pale for an indian."

"Kind of odd there was only one." the Major thought, "I wonder if he is alone, and if he is, why would he be alone? Usually, even the men go out in groups."

"Maybe he's an orphan." Momma gasped.

"Whoa, Audrey, Back up the wagon, we don't need an orphan indian in the family." The Major demanded, "There's no telling what he may, or may not do. We don't know enough about these savages to know what he has been taught. Besides, he couldn't know any english. How are you going to communicate with him?"

Momma ran her finger around the Major's ear and said, "Oh, I don't know, but he has already communicated with us, just by showing that he likes us. After all, he must have known that none of our soldiers were close enough to help. And he knew that me and Matthew were alone and helpless. He could have just watched us get butchered, but, he didn't. When you can explain the evil motive behind that boy coming to our rescue, we can talk about how savage he is, until that time, Matt. I will treat him like a friend."

The couple walked around the wagon and out of sight. Little Bear thought about this.

He wondered what he had just witnessed. The Major sounded very rough when talking to the private, but nice when he talked to Momma. He knew the family now, Momma, Yes Dear, and the Major.

Little Bear waited until all was calm, and most of the camp was sleeping to make his way to the lake. He decided to go around the camp, less chance of getting caught. He marveled at how many people, and things this tribe had. It seemed like a large camp. He was proud of himself. He had remained hidden from this tribe for a whole day. Not only that, he had not been noticed by the renegade he killed. He was even getting past the animals without being heard. He had somehow managed to become invisable. And there were so many things he had never seen before.

The wagons were like nothing he had seen. The horses were not normal in this country. He had seen one once that appeared to be wild, but his father told him these animals had never been seen here before. Little Bear was learning a lot, he thought as he drifted off to sleep.

Chapter
FOUR

Day 7 began as Little Bear watched the major leave the wagon. The sergeant had come to the wagon, and they seemed to be in a hurry. Momma was stoking the fire and stirring it up to make breakfast. Little Bear noticed that Yes Dear had not come to his side of the wagon since the attack. But, he could hear him playing near Momma. He remembered how his mother had made sure that he was close by when a renegade tribe was in the area.

The walker was coming toward the wagon. Little Bear noticed a wild cat nearing the area. He watched as the cat noticed the walker. She hid herself, but inched closer as the walker came nearer. The cat was preparing to attack, and the walker was totally unaware of the danger. The big cat pounced and growled. The walker was stunned, and dropped his fire stick, as the cat began tearing his clothes and his flesh. Little Bear threw his spear into the cat. The walker was screaming in pain, but got away from the cat. Then he looked up at where the spear came from. Soon there were men running from all directions to see what had happened. A fire stick went off, and the wild cat lay motionless.

"That little feller saved my life!" the walker claimed.

"What little feller?" the sergeant demanded.

"That little feller up in that tree." the walker answered as he pointed at Little Bear.

One of the men drew his fire stick and aimed at Little Bear.

"Don't you dare hurt that boy!" Momma screamed.

"He's a injun lady," The man responded, "can't trust no injuns." in any way.

"He has saved three lives so far," Momma yelled, "And I'll skin you alive if you hurt him in any way.

"At ease private!" the sergeant commanded, "He isn't gonna hurt us. That poor boy is scared to death."

Little Bear was frozen in time and space. His hiding was over. Now he would find out how this tribe treated strangers. Momma came near to the tree.

"It's okay little angel," She offered, "You can come down now."

Little Bear couldn't move if he wanted to. His muscles refused to act. There was more noise The major was running back to the wagon.

"What is the situation sergeant!" he demanded.

"Sir, this wild cat attacked private James, and apparently that young indian stopped it with that spear."

The sergeant related, "Private Conner was going to shoot him but, your wife started screaming and,"

"At ease, sergeant." The major interupted, "Audrey, what do you think you're doing?"

Momma was getting mad. "That private was going to shoot our angel." She stammered, "For helping another man of our company, who was in a pretty bad situation, and you are gonna yell at me!"

The major looked around and said, "Okay men, back to your duties, the excitement is over. Sergeant, get that man to the doctor."

"Yes, sir, Major." the sergeant answered, "Private Conner, you and Benjamin get this man to the doc."

"Yes, sergeant!" The private replied.

"Now," The major sighed, as he looked in the tree, "What do I do about you, angel boy?"

Momma began motioning for Little Bear to come down. "It's all right Angel, come on down."

Little Bear wasn't sure what was about to happen, but the words were soothing. The tone was soft.

He didn't feel threatened. He loosened up a little. His muscles began to move again.His heart stopped pounding. He knew he had to face them now. It was too late to run away. They did not act like they would hurt him. So he climbed down from the tree, and moved, cautiously, toward Momma.

Momma pointed to herself and said, "Audrey, can you say Audrey?"

Little Bear tried to figure out what was happening. He pointed at her and said, "Momma."

The major cringed and muttered, "Oh no, now what am I gonna do. She's gonna be wrapped around that boy's finger."

Momma tried again, "No, not momma, Audrey."

Little Bear answered back, "Momma," then he looked at the major and pointed, "Major." and then pointed in the boy's direction, and said, "Yes Dear."

Momma laughed, "This is going to take some time Matt."

The major answered, "I can see that, and I can see you plan on teaching this boy how to talk. I wonder how long he's been watching?"

A walker came by, Little Bear pointed and said, "Private."

Now the major was laughing. "Well, he has been here long enough to learn a few words at least."

Momma reached out for Little Bear. He flinched at first, not knowing what to expect.

"Come on, let's have some breakfast, Angel." She said as she led Little Bear to the fire.

"I better get back to the colonel." the major said, as he walked away, "He'll be wondering what's going on. Good-bye dear."

"Good-bye Matt." Momma said.

Little Bear learned fast. He could say oatmeal, and Audrey, and Matthew, he learned wagon, and tent, and fire. He noticed the stares from many in the camp. He heard the tones of anger from some and curiosity from others. Audrey kept calling him angel. And she always sounded kind and happy, except when one of the angry voices spoke up. Then she sounded angry, and she got pretty loud some times.

When they went down to the lake for water people stopped and stared too. Little Bear, Audrey, and Matthew with two buckets. Little Bear took a handful of water and drank, and watched as Audrey dipped the buckets and filled them. He reached for one, and someone slapped him hard.

"Don't you touch a white woman, injun!" the man said.

Little Bear felt tears start to well up in his eyes. He had fallen back and spilled the bucket. Audrey was up on her feet in a second, slapping at the man and yelling, "You leave Angel alone! He is just helping me with the water. What's the matter with you?"

"You gonna trust that savage to be that close to you, woman!" the man growled, and began to push her out of his way. Little Bear wasn't sure what to do, but he sure didn't like this man pushing Audrey at all.

The man came toward him swinging his fists. Little Bear was fast enough to dodge the man's attack, until a private pulled him away.

"That injun tried to kill me!" The man claimed Audrey yelled at the man. "You are a liar mister. You came up here and started beating up this boy for absolutely nothing. He didn't hurt you or me." She continued, "I was the one who brought him here and he hasn't tried to hurt anyone in this camp!"

"I tell ya he's a murderin injun, you better kill em now before it's too late." The man vowed.

"He doesn't look too dangerous to me." The private noted. "Are you alright, Mrs Dodd?"

"No! I am not!" Audrey declared, "A grown man picking on a boy, and then having the nerve to accuse this boy of attacking him, I am livid!"

"I tell ya lady, he's no good. He'll only bring trouble." the man ranted "Come on Morris." The private groaned, "Leave these people alone."

Audrey brought Matthew and Little Bear together and hugged them both, and clipped the buckets again, gave one to Little Bear and carried one herself back to the wagon.

Little Bear had felt hate before, from renegade tribesmen. What he didn't understand was why this man hated him.

Chapter
FIVE

There was a new noise in the camp. People were moving around. There was a sudden bustling all around the camp. The major came to the wagon. "Well, the colonel decided this river would make a good place to build. Looks like we'll be staying for a while."

"I thought he wanted to get farther away from the mountains." Audrey answered.

"No, he did a little scouting around the area. There's lots of water, enough wood to build a town, and a wall around the camp, and plenty of game to hunt." The major declared. "Colonel says, this is it."

Little Bear watched as the men began chopping trees, and clearing areas, marking off spaces, and setting up frameworks. He thought they were making quite a mess, and didn't understand this activity. They would not be burning this much wood. And they were trying to shape the wood.

Knocking off bark, using tools he had never seen to cut shapes in the wood. And tools that cut the trees fast. There was a long blade between two men and as they pushed it back and forth it cut the tree faster than Little Bear had ever seen a tree fall.

Audrey could tell Angel was caught up in the hub-bub. She would not be able to keep his attention. She watched Matthew playing. He didn't care what was going on, he just wanted to play. It was about time to start stoking the fire pit to cook anyway, she thought. She got up and began to put more wood on the fire and stoke it up. "Soon," She almost whispered, "We will be in a house instead of a wagon."

Little Bear was carving notch number 12 on his spear. The moon was so small, almost gone. He was nearly halfway through his ritual to become a man. He had learned of a new language, and he was beginning to understand it. He had watched a town grow up before his eyes. There was still much to do to get it done, but, he could see the houses and the stores, and walls taking form. He noticed the difference between his tribe and this tribe. His tribe was very careful with nature and took much time to do a project, while this tribe used nature, but got things done much faster. His tribe used the tools of their fathers that made the work harder and longer, and less sturdy, while this tribe used new tools that worked better. His tribe had less time to enjoy the life around them, and this tribe could finish a project and take time to enjoy more. His tribe had some good and some bad, but they were a family and stuck together, this tribe had some good and some bad, but they had fights among them, and could really be mean toward one another. These were different families, not a single family. They worked together to get things done, but then fought over who would benefit from it.

Little Bear had heard Morris talking about 'injuns'. He was the one that had slapped Little Bear and pushed Audrey down. He talked about killing every injun he could find, just because they were injuns.

"Don't need no other excuse." He had proclaimed, "They got that red skin, and act like the land is theirs, and I don't like em. Ain't no better than them darkies as far as I can see."

Little Bear didn't understand it all, but he knew now that he was what Morris called an injun, and he knew he didn't like it. And he knew, that man, and the one they called Chadwick were hateful. They hated because they wanted to hate.

The major was talking about a group of new people, coming to this new town.

"Probably come and settle for a while, and most will probably move on." He said, "We have become an out post, just a stop on the way west."

Audrey grew a little tense as she asked, "And what about your troops Matt? Will they need an escort to go on?"

"Well, not yet," The major replied, "they will already have an army escort with this group. May decide to transfer one or two, depending on how well they do getting here, but we won't be leaving, yet."

A knock came at the side of the wagon.

"Enter." The major said.

"Sir!" the sergeant said, as he opened the flap of the wagon, "Something is brewing down by the barn. I sent a man to the colonel's office. It sounds like Morris is stirring up trouble. He's got a bunch of men down there and they're drinking and getting worked up over the indian in your wagon."

"Thank you sergeant." The major replied, "Any idea how soon they'll be coming around?"

"I think they're on their way now, sir."

The major began to leave the wagon, as the voices closed in.

"We want the injun out here Dodd!" the voice yelled, "Or we'll come in and get em!"

The major looked at the mob that had made their way to his wagon.

"Do you really think you can just come over here, and I'll let you do whatever you feel like doing?" the major asked.

Morris stepped forward, "No! We figure you are gonna have to be taken out of the way first. You and that pretty lady of yours." He threatened.

The major began to get angry, "You know Morris, I've had just about all I can stand from you, and now you want to bring my family into your hatred?"

Morris smiled as he answered, "I've thought about what I could do with your woman if you were out of the way, and now you will be, you injun lover."

The major's first instinct was to plant his fist in Morris' mouth, but he knew he couldn't do that legally, yet. Morris waved for the group to close in on the major. There had to be eight or ten men in that crowd.

"That will do private." The colonel commanded, as the squad of soldiers surrounded the group. "It would appear you have way too much time on your hands gentlemen. Guards! Take them to the stockade! All of them."

One of the men cried out, "You can't do that! I'm not one of your soldiers!"

"Take them away," The colonel repeated, "Major, my apologies for allowing things to get this far out of hand. I had hoped, all of this nonsense would have blown over by now. But, there do seem to be some people, in this camp, that just refuse to allow for diversity in our town."

"Yes sir, The major replied, "But, we are surrounded by indians out here sir. If we don't find a way of living with them, many of them, and many of our own people will die. They can't really expect to just kill off the people that have lived here for generations."

"Yes, major, in fact, these people know where things are in this country. They have, and can be a very helpful asset in building this country." The colonel added, "They are a very good asset to learning about where we are, and where we should and should not be going."

"Yes sir, "The major replied.

"I guess we will just have to try to find adequate punishment for this bunch." The colonel added.

The major said, "Sir, not all of those men are that bad,"

"Yes major, I know, "The colonel interrupted, "It's mostly those two trouble makers getting the others all fired up, but they must know there are consequences for this kind of foolishness."

The colonel turned and went back to his office.

Little Bear had crept out the back of the wagon as the argument had ensued, deciding he would be much safer, for now, in the forest. He understood this group had come for him, and to do him harm.

He still didn't know what he had done wrong, to make these people so mad at him. And it appeared to him that Audrey and the major didn't either. After thinking for some time Little Bear decided it would be better to stay away for a while. He liked the major's family, and he would not bring harm to them. It would be better to stay away.

Chapter

SIX

The colonel sat in the center of the table. Two majors, and two captains on either side. Off to the right side of the tent there were four jury members. Two civilians and two privates. A sergeant sat as the prosecutor. The tent was full. Everyone wanted to see how this town would handle justice.

They brought in the civilians first. One by one they went before the panel and explained that they had not done anything, only walked with the group. And one by one they were told that this town would not be run by mob rule. That laws mattered. But, since they had done no real harm they would get off with just a warning and time served. Then they brought in the soldiers.

Private Elijah Jones, you are accused of inciting to riot, conspiracy to commit murder, threatening a superior officer, and public intoxication, how do you plead?" The sergeant demanded.

"Sir, "the private began," I got a little drunk, but I didn't lead the group, I just wanted to see what would happen."

A captain lean on to the table, "You are not a civilian, private. You were part of a group that threatened a superior. That is a court martial offense. Do you plead guilty or not guilty?"

"Well," the private thought, "I guess I'm guilty of bein part of the crowd, but I didn't do nothin bad I don't think I did none of them other things."

"Sergeant, What does the prosecution say?"

"Sir, We have six witnesses that saw this man as one of the men who showed obvious intent to attack Major Dodd, and his family. And we have three witnesses to the alcohol on private Jones' breath."

The prosecutor called his first witness.

"I call Private Owens." The sergeant ordered. The private took the stand.

"What was your duty private?" The sergeant demanded.

"I was actually off duty, sergeant, when Sergeant Winslow came in and said he needed as many of us as possible to follow him to stop a mob."

"And what did you see as you approached the scene?" The sergeant goaded.

"Well, sergeant, there was this bunch of guys threatening to kill some injun kid the major was takin care of in his wagon, and they was closin in on the major."

"And, what happened next? The sergeant demanded.

"The colonel ordered us to take the whole bunch to the stockade. So, we did." The private answered.

The sergeant nodded and said, "That is all I have for this witness sir."

"Private, do you have any questions of this witness?" The captain asserted.

"Yeah, I got a question," The private said, "Did you actually see me do or say anything to the major?"

The witness responded. No, I did not."

"That's all I got to ask." the private said.

The sergeant called all of his witnesses and asked, mostly the same questions, and got the same answers. And The private asked the same question and got the same answer. After weighing all of the evidence the major on the colonel's left side stood up.

"It is the finding of this court that this man is guilty of public intoxication, and threatening a superior officer, with intent to do bodily harm."

Then the colonel spoke up, "Under the circumstances, I feel the sentence of two weeks in the stockade, with daily labor, is an adequate punishment for you private, and a month's probation. That ought to be enough if you're smart."

Private Chadwick was next up, and the scenario was the same. The same witnesses, the same answers, and the same ruling.

Then came Private Morris. The sergeant began with his first witness.

"Will you tell this counsel if there is any difference between this member of the mob than the others, Private?"

"Yes sergeant, this man was the leader of the group. He was the one doing all of the threatening and inciting all of the rest." The private observed, "And I did see him grab the major's shirt."

The rest of the trial went steadily down hill for private Morris. The sergeant even brought three of the civilians that were part of the mob to testify that Morris was the one that started the whole thing. He was found guilty on all counts.

"Do you have anything to say before your sentencing Private Morris?" The captain asked.

"Yes I do, "Morris growled, "This is all just because of that stinkin injun! If the major hadn't brought that snake into the camp, none of this would've happened. Why ain't he bein tried fer what he done?

How come he gets off scot free? It ain't fair I tell ya!"

The colonel rose from his chair.

"Private Morris," He began, "You have been found guilty on all of the charges. And I find that this is not an isolated incident. There have been several times you have broken military regulations. You are hereby stripped of all rank, and will be dishonorably discharged. You will also spend five years in the stockade, at least until the jail is built, and then I want you out of this town."

There was silence for several minutes. People began to leave the area. Private Morris was taken to the stockade. There were whispers and speculations as the town went back to work.

Audrey was afraid. "Angel hasn't been back yet Matt." she moaned, "He may be too scared to come back ever again."

The major tried to console his wife. "We just don't know Audrey. We'll just have to wait and see. I know you liked him a lot, but there isn't much we can do. He knows more about this forest than we do. He could be anywhere."

"You don't understand Matt." She countered, "While we were coming here, after those first three fights we got into with the native tribes, I prayed for an angel to keep us from harm." she paused, "I don't want to lose our angel, honey."

The major stopped in his tracks, "You actually believe God sent this boy to us." He gasped.

"Yes I do," Audrey claimed, "Just look at all of the times he has saved us, and our friends."

"So thats why you call him Angel." Matt concluded, "I wondered about that. Baby, if he was sent by God he will be back, or, we don't need an angel any more."

The couple walked back to their wagon holding each other.

Little Bear had been curious about why the whole town had stopped everything they were doing to go to the big tent. But he didn't want get any closer to the place for fear of being seen. He recognized Chadwick and Morris being led in in chains, along with the eight others that were chained. He also noticed only three still wore chains when they left. Little Bear wanted to go back to see Audrey and the major, and Matthew, but, he didn't want to stir up any more trouble. He would lay low for a while and see what happened. He was also interested in their reaction to the deer he had killed and dressed for them for supper.

Audrey gasped when she saw the deer waiting to be cooked.

"Well dear, I don't think our angel has gone too far away." The major joked, "Looks like he is still helping out."

"Oh my," Audrey gulped, "What a sweet boy. You know I'll have to take some to him later."

The major laughed, "How do you know where he'll be?"

"I know where he found the food before, I bet he'll be there after I put it out there." Audrey answered

"I'll bet he'll be there."

Chapter
SEVEN

Little Bear carved the fifteen notch in his spear. The moon would
be black. If he could have seen it. It had been raining since just
before the sun had gone below the horizon. The camp was quiet.
Little Bear was full from the stew Audrey had left for him. All
seemed peaceful as Little Bear walked around the camp. Making sure
there were no reasons to worry this night. Another lesson his father
had taught him, to know what was close enough to harm you before
you sleep.

As he passed the fenced in area where the chained men had been
exiled, he heard whispers and stopped to see if he could find the talkers.
The guards were walking around the fence, and occasionally slipping
in the mud. Everything seemed to be okay, but Little Bear felt uneasy.
Something didn't seem quite right. Perhaps it was the sloshing around

of the guards, or maybe just the rain, but Little Bear felt something was wrong.

The sky lit up and a few seconds later he heard the boom of thunder. This night would not be easy he thought. Sleep would not come early. He passed a few wagons and heard voices of the new tribe, some of scared children, and of consoling parents, others of anger. The sky became bright as the day and the thunder shook the ground. The spirits set one of the structures on fire in the camp. Men came out of their wagons and began trying to stop the fire. There was shouting and screams, but the fire went out, and the people went back to their wagons. The spirits were angry now. The lightning came often, and the thunder was loud, and the rain began to pour down.

Little Bear was back in his hiding place, and watching the light show the spirits were giving him. So much light, and so much noise. Then he heard the splash of someone running. Little Bear looked in the direction of the splashing. As the sky lit up again, he saw Morris and Chadwick coming toward the major's wagon. He screamed.

"Major! Major!" And ran toward the wagon. Other voices began yelling. The major jumped out of the wagon in time to see the two men approaching. Little Bear ran straight into Chadwick and knocked him down, but Morris had gotten past him. Little Bear was in real trouble now. This man was a big man and he was angry. When Chadwick rose he looked at Little Bear and growled.

"Well, at last I get to get rid of a no good red skin." He grinned as he drew closer to Little Bear. Little Bear pulled his knife out of his pants, chadwick knocked it away from him. Chadwick's hands closed around Little Bear's throat.

"I'm gonna watch you die injun." He muttered.

There was the sound of a fire stick. Chadwick's hands relaxed, and he fell down beside Little Bear. The next thing Little Bear knew, the major was picking him up and carrying him to the wagon. The major was bleeding, and limping. But Little Bear noticed the body of Morris was lifeless.

"Well, our angel helped us again Audrey. "the major said.

"Oh my." Audrey gasped, "you're hurt. How bad is it?"

"Angel just needs to get his breath back, but I better go see doctor Southwell. I got a few pretty bad cuts on my side and leg." the major responded.

A sergeant came to the wagon, "What happened sir?"

"Sergeant help me get to the doc's tent."

"Yes sir Major, Private! You and corporal Jeffries get the major to the doc's tent. NOW! MOVE!"

The men came running to help, as men came to see what all the excitement was about.

"Okay, what happened private?" The captain demanded as he approached.

"Well, sir," The private responded, "I heard this yell for the major, and by the time I got back here this indian kid was bein strangled by the private. So, I shot him. And I looked around and the major was fighting with the other private, Captain."

"Are you quite sure the indian didn't attack the private, Private?"

"I don't think so sir, This private was spose to be in the stockade, and he was talkin about watchin the indian die, sir." The private related.

"Well, he did break out of the stockade, and it would appear there was intent to get revenge on the major, and the kid." The captain noted. "Sergeant! Get these bodies out of here, and organize a burial detail."

"Yes, sir." was the response.

"Damn, now I'll have to bother the colonel. I don't think he'll like this." The captain muttered.

The camp was bustling by this time. Audrey was comforting Little Bear and praising him and a person she called God. He didn't remember seeing anyone named God out there. Of course, he didn't know all of their names. Maybe that was the private's name. At any rate, he had never been treated like this before. He had been in a fight. His tribe would have left him to recover on his own, but these people acted like he had done some great deed. And, he was out of the rain.

The thunder and lightning had moved on, and the rain was not as hard. Matthew was asleep and Little Bear wondered if the major would be back soon. He had been gone a long time. But, he had been bleeding a lot. Audrey was still sniffling and talking about this God person. It finally struck Little Bear that she was talking to the spirits. This God person was the great spirit he had asked for help from many times. He reached for Audrey's shoulder and said.

"God help Angel, and Major, all good, Audrey." He said calmly.

Audrey began to cry.

"Oh Angel I hope so." She said, as she pulled Little Bear to her, and hugged him. "I truly hope so."

Suddenly it occurred to Audrey that this was the first time Angel had attempted making a sentence. He had repeated words, and had learned names, but this was the first he had put words together to try to communicate with her, and she understood every word. She thought, things would get easier now, if he can express himself, and understand her. This had been a big night.

Chapter
EIGHT

Mrs. Krause passed by the wagon every day to get water. Her daughter, Heidi, by her side. They seemed friendly enough, said hello, and sometimes stopped to ask a question, or just talk for a moment or two. Heidi always stayed on the other side of her mother when she saw Little Bear, until today.

"Hello Mrs. Dodd." the mother said as she set her bucket down. "How is your husband doing today?"

Audrey smiled, "Good day to you Mrs. Krause. Matt is recovering nicely, thank you. He should be getting back to near normal in a day or two. How is your family?"

"Otto says ve vill be moving into our haus in only a day or two." Mrs. Krause replied, in her thick German accent, "It vill feel so goot to be out of the wagon, finally."

"I'm glad to hear it. It looks like you will be one of the first." Audrey said.

"Ya," Mrs. Krause began, "My Otto said he vill come and help you vhen he ist done with our haus, but maybe you von't need him by then. I see you have soldiers helping."

Audrey smiled, "A bunch of Matt's company came to help after the fight last night. I think the colonel feels guilty that those two got away from the stockade."

Mrs. Krause laughed, "Ach, That is what they call a stockade. It is a wonder all of those men did not escape. I could even get out of that thing."

Heidi looked at Little Bear, "I heard you were a hero last night too Angel."

Little Bear didn't know what to do, so he waved his hand, "Hello." He managed.

Heidi giggled, "Hey momma, he can talk."

"Heidi!" Mrs. Krause exclaimed, "It is not nice to tease the boy."

Heidi looked up at her mother, "I wasn't teasing momma, this is the first time I've ever heard him Speak."

Little Bear watched and listened. He wasn't sure he understood it all, but, he understood that Heidi was talking about him, and she sounded friendly. And she looked pretty, with her curly blond hair, and big blue eyes. He decided he liked her, and would show her he could talk.

"Soon Angel talk good, you see." He sputtered, and smiled.

Audrey looked at Angel, and then at her guests, "I think he's learning pretty fast. He is a bright young man."

Little Bear perked up. This was the first time any of these people had called him a man. He was always called a boy, or a kid before. He had proven himself here. For these people he had passed the test of manhood he thought.

Audrey and Mrs. Krause talked for a few more minutes, while Heidi and Angel traded glances and smiles. Heidi waved at Angel as she picked up her bucket to leave. Angel waved back, and watched as they walked away. Angel decided he was doing well with this tribe. There were still many he knew did not like him, but he seemed to be getting more friends as time went by.

Little Bear thought about Wild Flower. She was not as pretty as this Heidi was. And her hair was dark, and so were her eyes. Her hair was straight. Wild Flower did not giggle like this girl, but she was the prettiest girl in the tribe, that wasn't already spoken for. Little Bear wondered why he was comparing the two. Heidi was not of his tribe. She would probably not want to be Little Bear's woman.

What was the matter with him? But, she was pretty, and she made Little Bear feel funny inside.

Little Bear began to wonder why the spirits had led him to this new tribe. His mother had told him the spirits guide you toward what you are to become. And his father had said that he would find his place in this trial, that what he would learn about life and being a brave at this time would teach him what his role would be in the tribe. And the wise elder of the tribe, who had determined he was ready to go through this trial, had said he would learn who he was by how he handled living in the forest. That he would leave as a child, and come back as a brave, able to do the things of a man.

Why was he thinking of these things now? Little Bear was confused. He decided to go out into the forest to think for a while. He got up and turned to Audrey, and smiled, and walked into the forest.

What was he suppose to become? Little Bear thought. How was this adventure creating his future? He wasn't learning to hunt bear, or buffalo, or even deer. Though he had proven his ability to hunt deer, that was not what he was learning. He already knew that. His father had taught him how to catch deer, and rabbits, and fish. And what about these new people? Why did some hate for no reason? What was he learning from them?

Little Bear had been walking for some time before he thought about turning back to get back to his place before night would fall. He still wasn't sure what he was learning. He came upon a brave making a fire pit. He recognized the the tribal colors and atributes, but he knew he had never seen this brave before. The brave looked at Little Bear.

"Come and sit with me Little Bear." the brave said, as he motioned toward a tree stump.

Little Bear felt a fear inside himself.

"Who are you? And how do you know me? I have never seen you before." Little Bear asked.

The brave smiled and said, "I've known you since before your birth Little Bear. I've watched you grow, and have been waiting for you to come to me. You have finally come. Now, you need answers, now I can help."

"I don't understand. Who are you? Little Bear demanded.

"Who I am is not important. Who you are becoming is what is important." The brave said, "You are between two peoples. You were raised to be a great brave and a mighty hunter, and now you are learning of a different way to live. And you are here wondering what you are, and what you are learning."

Little Bear sat quietly wondering how this brave knew so much about him.

"In your tribe you knew some who liked you and some who did not like you. It did not matter you needed to get along, for the sake of the tribe. "The brave smiled, and continued, "Now you have found people who will not get along with you, just because of who you are, and what you represent to them. Some would kill you just because you were born to your tribe, in this land, to your parents. And you will learn that there are some of your people that would kill these new people, just because they look and act differently than you."

"But, why do people hate for no reason?" Little Bear asked.

The brave looked at Little Bear's eyes and answered, "There are many reasons for hatred Little Bear. Some because of greed, some for power, some for fear, some for envy, and even some for love. The one that tried to kill you, hated because you were not his kind. He looked at you as he would a snake or a coyote, as less than a man. He would see any man who was not like him in the same way. That is what killed him, he died long before his heart stopped beating, long before you came to his camp. He hated because he knew how life should be, and no one else does what he knew was right. There is no tribe that does not have haters among it's people. Those who grew up learning to hate, either from parents who taught to hate, or could not show love, or family that treated them as bad people, or some of the other things I've already told you."

Little Bear thought about what the brave said. He remembered Gentle Rain, the boy who had teased him and pushed him around for so many years. He had this hate inside him. Little Bear knew of no reason for the hate. He was not a lonely child, and his parents showed much love toward him it seemed. But still, Gentle Rain was a mean boy. This was the one Little Bear had fought with on more than a few occasions. He remembered how he had wondered why Gentle Rain would start a fight knowing he would be punished afterward, whether he won or lost. And Little Bear remembered that Gentle Rain got punished often.

"There is more Little Bear." The brave continued, "You have seen the differences in the way these people live, the clothes they wear, the tools they use, the food they eat, even how they celebrate.

You have studied how they build with the tools they use, and how little they care about the forest and and the life in the forest. That they not only cut down trees, but pull out the roots to clear the land. And the houses they build are much sturdier than the huts your tribe make. While your people take great care for the land, and only make temporary huts, and the houses they do make are not as strong. Their tools are not as fast or as easy to use. But in the end, your people are proud to live with nature. Proud of their lifestyle. They can pass on their respect for the ancestors that taught them, and have kept their tribes alive, but there is very little change. These new people do not show the respect for the old ways, but find ways to do the same things faster and easier. It is much faster and easier to point a fire stick and shoot, than to throw a spear, they have longer range, and do not take as much effort. It is much easier to make a tool to cut a tree faster, than to use only an ax, and need to sharpen it often. And even you have seen that change must happen, in the sky, in the land, and in the water. Change is everywhere.

Little Bear thought about watching his father drag dead wood from the forest to build the shelters they would live in, and how when they came back the next year he would have to build it again. And the houses the new tribe were building that would stand for many years. It occurred to him that his mother would work very hard to clean the skins they wore, and how the women cleaned the clothes on the wooden boards. Took less time, and the clothes seemed cleaner. And the fact that if any of the people of his tribe had showed any care for him, besides his mother, after he fought with Gentle Rain they would have been given a talk on the traditions of the elders, and the ways of nature. Every man must be able to defend himself.

"But, which is the better way?" Little Bear asked.

The brave shook his head, "It is better to keep those things that are good, and change those things that can be changed. It is better to live with nature, and grow with new findings. There is nothing wrong with remaining true to the traditions of your people that do not hold you back. But if you do not learn of the new things you can do, your people will be left behind. You have seen how the renegades attacked with their arrows and spears and did very little damage to the new people, with their fire sticks. And if they had not stopped their attack they would have all died, and the new people would have had only minor damage." He smiled and added, "You have been taught to grow with the land.

Well, the land is being changed. And the new people are changing it. They have skills and knowledge to make life different than what it is now. The land is growing, are you growing with it? No way that man chooses is perfect. Do what is best."

There was silence for a short time. Little Bear finally rose, and turned to the brave, nodded, and began to walk away. He looked back to see the brave stoking the fire, and waved as Little Bear left.

Chapter
NINE

It was the nineteenth day of Little Bear's trial. The sun was out. Many wagons had been emptied into the new houses that were close to completion. And many new areas for houses were being cleared.

The town was beginning to take shape. On the east end there were many tents that housed the soldiers, and on the west were the headquarters, and corrals, and a new stockade, and a building that would soon house the soldiers. The south had the lake, and the north, the forest.

Two men had come in from the east and were talking about the wagon train that would be passing through before nightfall. It was, apparently, almost as big a group as was already there. But they would only stay for a day or two and go on west. They spoke of indian attacks on the way there that had slowed the train down. They said several settlers had been killed in the attacks, but the rest had made it through.

"Looks like some of em got a hold of some rifles." The scout warned, "But we still got the best of em."

Little Bear looked at Audrey, "Rifles?" he asked.

The scout pulled his rifle out of it's holster, and held it out toward Little Bear, "Rifle." He said.

"Who get rifles?" Little Bear prodded.

The scout leaned over toward Little Bear and said, "Somehow those indians up in the mountain pass got a hold of some rifles. And they must've been taught how to load and shoot em too. Last time I saw an indian with a rifle, he had to use it like a club. Had no idea how to load it up, or shoot it." The scout squinted at Little Bear, "Say, you look like an indian boy."

Audrey interrupted, "And you look like you need a bath, and a shave. Mister, we don't need anybody starting any trouble today."

"No ma'am, ain't tryin to start no trouble, just takin notice. I know some pretty good indians myself.

It's only the bad ones that's the problem. This one here looks about the right age fer becomin a brave."

The scout pondered, then he spoke in Little Bear's tongue, "Are you doing your trial, brave?"

Little Bear felt a twinge of fear that this man could talk in his own language, but noddoed, "I am"

Little Bear knew this man was showing respect toward him by calling him a brave. He just wasn't sure what the man had in mind. The scout bowed his head and said, "I wish you the honor of a great warrior. What are you called?"

Little Bear scowled and answered, "Little Bear."

The scout laughed, which made Little Bear uncomfortable, and the scout said, "You can no longer be Little Bear, you must now be Great Peace maker."

Little Bear perked up. This was a great compliment, and a great name for a brave.

Audrey wasn't sure what to think of all of this. She had no idea what the two were saying. But, she noticed the gleam in Angel's eye. He seemed to be okay with whatever the man said. The scout moved on toward the corral. The other scout turned around and headed back to the wagon train.

"Nice man." Angel offered.

Audrey smiled and said, "If you say so, Angel."

"He talk nice to Angel." Angel confirmed, "Show honor."

"He could still use a bath and a shave." Audrey mumbled, and then giggled.

It was much later when the bustling began on the east side of the town. Little Bear climbed his lookout tree to see what was going on. There were soldiers riding in and taking defensive positions and yelling for back-up. The soldiers in the tents came running out and joined the incoming riders. Soon the first wagons appeared at full gallop. The arrows and spears still stuck in the wagons, and the canvas.

The wagons rolled through the town slowing as they reached Audrey's house, but continuing towards the headquarters. Then came the sounds of the rifles. The air became full of smoke from the wagons, and the rifle fire.

Little Bear watched as many men both soldiers and braves fell. He knew what war looked like.

He had watched the renegade tribes fight like this, and his own tribe fight back. He had watched his father fighting, and killing many braves. And he watched some of his uncles die. He understood why his father fought to protect his home and his family, he never understood why other tribes wanted to attack his home and family. They had migrated up and down these same paths for generations. Some years were beautiful and peaceful. Other years, other tribes would attack. Some times not many got hurt, other times many would die. He had only known the cause one time, when Wailing Coyote had taken a girl from the renegade tribe, and they came for him. He remembered that after the war, the chiefs talked. Wailing Coyote was brought before the tribe and killed in front of the renegades. That brought peace for that year.

It occurred to Little Bear that after all of the spears and arrows that had been used in that battle only Wailing Coyote died. There had been wounds, but no one else had been killed. The spirits only required Wailing Coyote for the wrong he had done.

Little Bear saw the indians spreading around the town in the woods. The soldiers moved too.

And more soldiers from the west side of town were spreading around the town too. He wondered how long this war would last. He could already see that the indians would not win. The soldiers could shoot better, and reload faster, and had better protection.

There was a scream and a woman came runniing out of a house dragging a boy.

"They got my husband!" She screamed.

Soldiers went in and dragged out the body of an indian and one of the settlers that had been stabbed.

The woman cried as they took both bodies away.

Little Bear saw an indian sneaking under his tree. For the first time in his trial he questioned what to do. Should he help the families he had made friends with, or should he help his own people?

His mind raced back to the brave in the forest.

"No way man chooses is perfect, do what is best."

The indian was heading toward Heidi's house. This family had done nothing wrong. Otto did not fight.

Nor did Mrs. Krause, and he liked Heidi. Little Bear knew he would have to either do something quickly, or let these people die. He could not let this family die. He scurried down the tree as fast as he could. As he reached the ground he found another brave sneaking up on him. The brave pounced just as Little Bear was raising his spear. His spear caught the brave in the air. It was all happening so fast.

He ran to the Krause' house. The brave was climbing into the hole in the wall and stabbing as he crawled through it. Little Bear stabbed the attacker, and pulled him back out of the hole. As he turned the attacker around a rifle sounded and the brave sank down to the ground. There was another crack from a rifle, and everything went dark.

Little Bear's head was throbbing. He felt a cool dampness on his forehead, and he heard the voices of Mrs. Krause and Heidi.

"He's gonna be alright Heidi," Mrs. Krause was saying, "It only scraped his skull. Looks like he's coming around finally."

"Is daddy gonna be alright momma?" Heidi asked.

Mrs. Krause answered, "Vell, he von't be doing much with his left arm for a vhile, but, it vould have been much vorse if Angel hadn't come vhen he did."

"Ya, "Otto added, "he ist a goot boy."

Little Bear opened his eyes to see the cloth Mrs. Krause was using to cool his wound. He saw Heidi behind her mother with tears on her face. She smiled as she saw Little Bear's eyes open. She looked down at him, and sighed.

"He is our guardian angel."

Mrs. Krause leaned down and kissed his forehead.

"Yes dear, he seems to be right where we need him."

"He's wonderful." Heidi cooed, as she softly rubbed his arm.

Chapter
TEN

Little Bear knew the moon wasn't right. It was almost full. He wondered how long he had been asleep. It seemed everyone knew what he had done. People from around the town came by and greeted him now. He had even been visited by a soldier who said how sorry he was for not recognizing him, and asking for forgiveness.

The Krause's were treating him very well. He had never seen anyone treated as well as they were treating him. He was eating three times a day. When he would try to get up they would watch him closely and steady him if he wobbled a little. He was still off balance, but not too bad. And Heidi only left his side to fetch the water.

He asked, "How many daytimes I here?"

"About four." Heidi answered.

That meant it was day twenty three, Angel thought. Seven more days to go, and it would take five days to get back to the tribe, (if he took the same route he came by). He knew he could get around, but he knew he was not ready for a five day journey yet, besides, he wasn't ready to leave Heidi yet. She had been very close to him. She felt soft when she touched him. And once when he lost his balance he had fallen against her, and she had put her arms around him and held him for what seemed like a long time.

And it felt good, very good.

"Angel need to walk." He stated, "Sitting too long, need to think in forest."

"Okay,' Heidi said, "we will go for a walk."

She headed for the door and Otto spoke.

"You don go too far Heidi. You stay close to haus."

"Yes Papa." She answered, "we won't go too far."

After a few minutes Heidi reminded Angel they were not to wander too far. Then she stopped and asked.

"Angel, do you like me?"

"Yes, Angel like Heidi much." He answered.

"I like you too Angel, a lot." She cooed, "You're so strong, and sweet."

Angel wasn't sure what to say now, he had never been called sweet before.

"Candy sweet, not Angel. "He countered.

Heidi giggled. Angel watched her smile. She looked so pretty, and so open to him. He admired her hair, and the yellow dress she wore accented the blond locks. Those beautiful blue eyes. He could look at her for hours, he thought. She wrapped her arms around him, and kissed him, right on the mouth. Angel moved away from her. He didn't know what to do, he had never heard of this behavior before, but somehow, he felt guilty. He felt something else too. He wanted her.

She skipped away heading back toward the house, "We really should go back, Angel." She laughed.

"Papa will wonder what we are doing."

Angel ran after her, and caught her by her waist, turned her around and tried to kiss her back.

He knew he was clumsy, but this was the first time he had ever done this. And Heidi wasn't upset, in fact, she seemed to be encouraging him. Her arms went around his neck, and he felt her body press against his, and she stayed pressed against him for a time. When she pushed herself away, she headed back to the house. Angel followed. Angel was confused. He had waited until all of the family was asleep to sneak out of the house. He couldn't sleep. He kept remembering how he felt with Heidi's arms around him. But, he could not take her back to his tribe. She is an outsider. They would never accept her. They may think he stole her away like Wailing Coyote. That would mean his death, from his own father. But, Angel wanted this girl. And what about Otto? Would he accept Angel as Heidi's man? Could Angel fit in with these pale skinned people? But Heidi was so pretty, and so soft, and so willing.

Angel was so caught up in his thoughts that he hadn't heard the footsteps.

"Angel, where are you?"

Angel looked toward Heidi's voice.

"Why you come?" He stammered as he watched her approach. He could see the outline of her figure through the light fabric of her gown.

"I heard you leave," She cooed, "I wanted to be with you again."

"This not good." Angel said, "Father and mother be angry for us."

Heidi sauntered up into Angel's arms, "I don't care, I want to be with you." Heidi whispered as she pressed against him again, "You feel so good."

Angel pushed her away, "No Heidi!" He commanded. "Is not right to do this without father and mother know what we do!"

"He ist right, Heidi." Otto's voice commanded. "And if you go to see a boy in secret, you should not wake your father as you go. Get back to the haus."

Otto looked at Angel. "Thank you for being a gentleman, Angel." Otto sighed, Perhaps one day it may be alright, but not like this."

ELEVEN

Thoughts were racing through Angel's mind too fast. There were too many things happening all at once. Why do these people take so long, (Heidi), to make a shelter? Their shelters are more solid.

(Heidi) than the huts he had lived in. He thought. Why do some want to kill other people? Why was he here (Heidi), anyway? Why did the spirits lead him to, (Heidi).

Angel stopped and looked around. He wondered how long he had been walking, and where he was. He knew he was tired. He knew he would sleep soon. He noticed a fire through the bushes. He crept around to see who might be there. He saw an indian brave once he recognized him he came out to talk.

"Why are you still here?" He asked.

The brave smiled, "Where should I be, Little Bear?"

Little Bear smiled and pondered, "Yes where should I be? And why am I here?"

The brave snickered, "Because you cannot be where you are not."

Little Bear chuckled, and added, "Right now I am not sure if I am where I am."

The brave became serious, and stated, "But, you are. And you could not be anywhere else. Only you can live your life. Only you will see the things you will see. Like every man before you, no one can go through what you go through. When you tell your story, there will be many who will listen, and many will understand, but none will feel what you felt."

Little Bear thought about what he heard.

The brave continued, "When you must decide quickly, you do what you feel is best." He began, "You are not truly deciding, you are reacting. You decide where to camp, you react when a bear attacks you.

You decide who you like, and who you hate, you react when someone likes you back. You decided to watch these new people, you reacted by defending them when danger came."

"But, I still don't know if I did right or wrong." Little Bear complained, "Should I have

turned on my own kind? Should I have allowed that family to live? How do I convince myself that it is right to do harm to my own skin to defend one who is not of my skin?"

The brave poked at the fire, "In the heat of battle you react according to what you see as right.

You have taught yourself what to look at to determine right from wrong. You learned that taking a woman that you should not take can lead to death, and you reacted. And you learned that some people can hate for no good reason. Now, when you have no time to decide, you react to what you have taught yourself is the right thing to do."

Little Bear felt his eyes getting heavy. He looked over at the brave again and said, "Then, I did right."

"You did what Little Bear decided was the right thing to do." The brave insisted. "You have already experienced the results of your decision, was the result good or bad?"

"It felt good to have the family, and Heidi take care of me, but, what will be the result from my family if they know?"

Little Bear's eyes closed as he slumped to the ground and fell asleep.

The sun had been out for some time when Little Bear woke up. He looked around. There was no sign of the brave, there was not even any sign that there had been a camp fire there. Had he been dreaming that whole conversation? He figured out which way to go to get back to the town. There was still much to digest of what had been happening to him the last few days. He understood now why it was called a trial. He was being tested on things he had never imagined could happen.

As he approached the town he heard the commotion, something was happening that he was missing. He heard rifles firing, and whoops and screams. It sounded like another battle had begun. He decided to move slowly so he would not be seen. There was a brave stumbling toward him. He had been shot. He was bleeding. As the man drew closer Little Bear began to recognize his face.

"Gentle Rain!" He stammered, "Why are you here?"

"Little Bear, "Gentle Rain groaned, "I did not know you had joined us."

"I did not know any of our people were here." Little Bear gasped. "This is far from our home."

Gentle Rain groaned and said, "Yes, you have not gone back yet, have you? You have not seen what the pale skins have done to our home."

"The pale skins were at our home? Little Bear muttered.

"They attacked without warning. By the time the tribe knew they were there, many were already dead.

Those who ran lived, those who fought died." Gentle Rain panted, his breathing became harder and faster, "This is where they must have come when they left our home."

Little Bear grabbed Gentle Rain's shoulder. "How long ago did this happen, how long?" He demanded

Gentle Rain began to slump down to the ground. "Six days Little Bear, six days." He gasped, his head dropped down and his body went limp in Little Bear's grip.

Little Bear needed to see what was happening in the town. He had to know what had happened there first. He considered as he made his way to the town, six days, that would have been 2 days before the wagon train had gone through the town. By the time he got there the fighting had ended and bodies lay strewn around the town, inside and out. The major was ordering men to clean up the area, and get the wounded to the doctor. Little Bear came to him.

"What happen here Major/" he asked.

The major looked at Angel and said, "Those braves took us by surprise. Crept in through the trees and butchered a bunch of towns people before we had time to react. We have got to finish putting up that wall."

Angel went to the Krause' house and knocked, as he had learned to do. Mrs. Krause opened the door. Tears were streaming down her face.

"They killed my Otto!" She cried, "I should not have gone for vater so early. If only I had vaited a little longer, I vould have been there. Vhat vill ve do now? How vill ve live vis out Otto?"

Angel looked inside the house. Heidi was sitting and crying too. Mrs Krause put her arms around Angel and cried. Angel held Mrs. Krause for a few minutes trying to decide what he should do.

It was wrong that these people had paid such a price for what others had done, but, it had been wrong for the pale skins to attack his tribe for no apparent reason. He could understand his people getting revenge for being so brutally attacked, but, the settlers they killed were not the ones that were responsible for that attack. And most of those who might have been responsible were already at least two days from the town.

Angel thought that he should see what had happened to his family, but he was worried that if he left again more might die. He had not been there this time. He may have stopped the mayhem if he had been there. He may at least have saved Otto.

As he walked away from Mrs. Krause he felt tears welling up in his eyes. It was not right for a brave to cry he thought. That is for women and girls, not for a brave. He went back to his hiding place determined to not act like a girl, but, the tears fell. He began walking again. He must not allow himself to have so much feeling over this event. A brave overcomes his emotions, he thought. But he still could not stop the anguish he felt, for the Krause family, or Gentle Rain, or his trible.

Chapter
TWELVE

It had only taken Little Bear three days to get back to where his tribe had been. As he entered at the site he looked around the area. Many of the huts had been destroyed. He found no one there. But, there were no bodies around either. Some had lived, but, they had moved on down the trail of migration. They would not stop here again. He must find them. He must know what had happened to Wild Flower and so many others he had grown up with. He looked for signs to make sure which way they had gone. There were not many that had gone. The tracks were not as cluttered as when there were many. And there were mostly soft footprints. Little Bear knew that meant most of the survivors were young.

It had taken four more days to catch up with the tribe. Gray Wolf had become chief now. There were not many older people left to lead the tribe. There were no braves left, only women and children, and a few old men. Little Bear asked Gray Wolf what had happened to Wild Flower. Gray Wolf looked down at the fire and said.

"The pale skins came and destroyed our camp Little Bear. They killed all of the braves and many women. Wild Flower was taken with some other girls, we have not seen them since then."

Little Bear thought about that for a moment. "Then she still may be alive." He managed.

Gray Wolf lifted his head slightly and said, "She may still be breathing, but, by now she is dead to us.

She has been shamed if not killed Little Bear."

Little Bear shuddered for a moment and considered, she was not with the wagons that had come into the town. And, he had not looked for anything outside of the camp. She must be somewhere, he thought. "I must know what happened to Wild Flower." He decided, "I must see if I can find her."

"No Little Bear." Gray Wolf replied, "If she is still alive, she is a slave to the pale skins. You cannot save her now."

I will not know that, if I do not find her."Little Bear argued, "She cannot be with the people I saw at the town I saw, and you did not see her die. If she is alive I must find her. She was to be my woman."

Gray Wolf looked up at Little Bear, "Truly, you are a brave now. You have become, Avenging Spirit."

Little Bear considered the title he had been given, but only for a second. He thought, "I must be on my way, it has already been too long since she was taken."

"May the spirits speed you on your way Avenging Spirit." Gray Wolf offered.

When Little Bear got back to the camp site the moon was nearly gone. He had passed the time of his trial. He had been given his brave name. He considered that name, Avenging Spirit, and that the pale skins had named him Angel. From all they had said about him, he wondered how close those two names were. But the pale skins called him a guardian angel, a protector, Gray Wolf had named him Avenging

Spirit, one that repays evil deeds. He wondered if he could be a protector and an avenger too.

He decided he should be Angel, angel is a spirit. He would be Angel from now on.

When morning came Angel searched for tracks of the pale skins. He found the tracks of the horses. He began following the tracks. After a while he found the body of a pale skin, with an arrow still in it. He studied the arrow, and knew it was the way his father had made his arrows. His father died fighting, he thought, and had killed at least one pale skin. He went back to following the trail of the horses.

The sun was still in the sky when Angel came upon the camp of the pale skins. He looked around the camp. He saw two men sitting and putting sticks in their rifles. He remembered that was how the rifles were cleaned. He thought back to all he had learned from the soldiers about their rifles.

There had to be a substance called gun powder packed into the barrel, and a thing called a bullet, the cap that had to spark the powder. There was more, but those were the things Angel could remember He saw the keg that would hold the powder. Angel remembered another thing, the powder is what made the noise, and the fire, and made the bullet fly.

There was another man walking out of a tent. There were only four tents Angel noticed. If there were two in each tent, that meant eight men. And there had to be room for the girls in one of those tents he thought. That brought the number down, by at least two. There were not many men in this group.

As he looked around he saw a box with rifles in a wagon, and more powder. The horses were under some trees. He counted ten horses. Again Angel tried to figure out what he would be up against. Ten horses, seven men counting the dead one. A wagon. There should not be more than seven men in this group, he concluded. Two horses for the wagon, seven horses for the men still there, and one for the dead man.

Angel knew he was guessing, he couldn't be sure. Two more men came from around some trees heading toward the two cleaning the rifles. Five so far Angel thought. So he moved around the area, being careful not to make noise. When he finally got close enough to hear he listened intently.

"How much longer we gonna stay here? I thought we waz gonna go to a town soon. Wez almost outta booze."

"Now don't get all fired up there Sam. The fishin is great here and they's deer all over. We can go to the town after we're sure all the fightin is done."

"You know better than that, Bert, Them injuns done lost that fight more than a week ago."

"Did ya ever think somebody might a told em where they got them rifles? Be a good idea to give plenty of time to think we ain't here yet."

"Say Bert, where is we gonna sell them girls? I say we should be able to have a little fun with em now."

"There's other injuns that'll trade blankets and skins fer em. Git to a traders shack and probably get ten or twenty dollars for em, but they gotta be pure. Try to pass em off as somethin they ain't could get us killed. And they won't give hardly nothin fer just a slave."

Angel understood enough to know he didn't have much time to decide what to do. It must be tonight he thought. But How? He continued tracing the camp. Looking to see if he could find where. the girls were. He finally heard some moans and crying from one tent. One of the men got up and walked over to the tent. He pulled out one of the girls. Her wrists and ankles were tied. He loosened her ankles, and led her down to the pond that the two men had come from. A few minutes later he brought her back. He said something before he left them alone.

Angel crept back around the camp, to the tent where the girls were. He marveled at how easily he was able to get around without anyone noticing. He was very good at sneaking he decided. He heard a noise that was out of place. One of the men was scraping something. It was one of the things the pale skins cooked their food in. Angel could not go to the front of the tent without being seen, but, he could sneak up to the back of the tent. He lifted the edge just enough to see inside. There were three of his friends, Wild Flower, Soft Blossom, and Cactus Flower.

Angel crept back into the forest to decide what to do. He decided he could find a way to get rid of these pale skins and rescue his friends. He came around to the wagon, he waited until he was sure no one would notice. The men had begun to eat when he took a keg of powder off the wagon. He quietly brought it back into the forest. He found the plug and removed it. He crawled into the camp behind the tents and began to spread the powder from tent to tent. He listened intently to the men to notice if something changed. He knew his life depended on whether he was discovered.

He heard laughter, he backed back into the forest, and looked to see what had happened. The men were passing around a bottle. Angel knew he was almost done spreading the powder. He had to finish. The sun was down, there was still some light but the darkness had set in. It would not be long now, Angel thought. But, he waited. When he finished spreading the powder he was back at the wagon.

He poured powder all over the wagon, and the other kegs.

The pale skins went to their tents, after a time. The moon was gone this night. The darkness was Angel's friend. He crept into the tent where the girls were. When they saw Angel they began to talk.

But he kept them quiet as he untied the ropes that held them, and motioned for them to go into the forest. He came out of the tent. He went to the place where the horses were tied and loosed their ropes too. They were away from the camp so they should be alright Angel thought. He went to the fire and took the keg that the pale skins had been using to load their rifles, and took it back to the trail of powder and made a trail from the trail he had already made to the fire. He threw powder into the fire.

Angel ran back into the forest, as the fire followed the trail to the tents. He met up with the girls just before the fire got to the first tent. He pulled the girls away from the camp, he knew he did not want to be too close when the fire got to the wagon. The firstt tent began to burn, just before the fire made it to the second tent. And soon the third began to burn. As the third began to burn, men ran out of the first tent yelling, "Fire! We're on fire!"

The pale skins were confused. They did not know what was happening. One tried to grab a bucket to go to the pond, but just as he began to run, the fire reached the wagon. The blasts knocked Angel down and destroyed the entire camp. Angel looked to see if any of the pale skins were coming after them. Not one was standing, and none were moving. The horses had come toward Angel and the girls. He only found six, but, he and the girls would move much faster now, and if the pale skins survived, they would be slow now.

It occurred to Angel he had not eaten since he had the berries he picked that morning, but it was too dangerous to stop now. Wild Flower came to Angel's side and said, "I thought I would not see you again. And you saved us."

"I could not have lived not knowing what happened to you, and when I found you were alive, I had to try to free you." Angel answered.

'the spirits are with you Little Bear. "she noted, "You will be a great brave, and I a good squaw."

"Gray Wolf said I am now Avenging Spirit." Angel announced. "And I am not sure where I will be now. The spirits have changed my path. I would have had you as my woman before my trial, but, now there is more that I must do, and another woman I feel much for."

"But there are only the three of us left for you, Avenging Spirit," Wild Flower complained, "And you said you would never want Cactus Flower, or Soft Blossom."

"I have met another." Angel said, "She made me feel differently than you do. I will have to decide between the two of you. And I will have to decide to stay with the tribe, or go to her."

Wild Flower faded back with the other girls and the rest of the trip back to the tribe was quiet.

Chapter

THIRTEEN

There was much celebration when Angel got the girls to the tribe. They danced and sang around the camp all day and into the night. Gray Wolf even danced a little. When the children and the girls went to their tents, Gray Wolf sat down with Avenging Spirit, and asked, "What will you do now. Wild Flower said you have another life."

"I am not sure what the spirits want me to do." Angel claimed. "I know I am needed here, but, I also am needed there. Wild Flower is suppose to be mine, but, there is a more beautiful woman with the pale skins that has given me stronger feelings."

"A pale skin woman!" Gray Wolf shouted.

"I went where the spirits led me." Angel proclaimed, "I learned much from the pale skins. Their teaching showed me how to save our girls. And many of their ways would make it easier for our tribe to live better lives. These horses make them faster, and their tools make their work faster and easier than our ways."

Gray Wolf grimaced, "They have murdered our people. They have plundered our land."

Angel responded, "Only a few have bothered us. Most pale skins are like our tribe. And even you have told me there will be good and bad in every tribe. The ones that attacked our tribe were not with the people of the town of this woman."

"But she is not of the same skin as you and I." Gray Wolf argued, "You cannot become a pale skin, And she cannot become of our skin. This is a barrier that should not be breached."

"I have seen the hatred some pale skins have for us. And I have seen the hatred our people have for them. I have also seen that many care more for your works than what skin you wear. "Angel countered, "And they are a caring people. There are bad ones, but just like me and Gentle Rain. We could not act good together. We argued and we fought. He did not like me and I did not like him. We tried to stay apart and as long as we were apart we were both good. As long as you stay away from the bad people whether they are of your own tribe, or any other tribe, things can be good."

"But they did not even give us a chance to be good, Avenging Spirit." Gray wolf said."We had no chance to be bad or good to them."

Angel became very serious, as he began," Gray Wolf,, I have seen what the pale skins can do. They can kill more braves faster than anything I've ever seen. Their fire sticks can kill from much longer than our spears or arrows. And more of them keep coming to our land. They will overtake us one way or another. If we do not become friends we will die some day, and they will have our land anyway. If we fight them we lose, If we keep away from them, we lose, if we join them we continue with the tools that make life easier. I helped some of them through their troubles and became good in their eyes. Why would I give up the chance to learn of a better life, and stay in the ways of our ancestors, and probably be killed by the bad ones."

"The bad ones will kill you either way." Gray Wolf noted, "They will not care what tribe you are with only that you are not a pale skin. And we need you here. There are no braves able to do the work of a brave in our camp. And what of the women? Where will they find a brave to give us more children.

How will we survive without a future?"

"I must follow where the spirits lead me."Angel stated, "I must think about all of these things and decide. I do not know which way to go yet."

The next morning Angel prepared to leave the camp. Wild Flower begged him to stay, but he was determined to go.

"I must find out what the spirits want me to do, and I do not know yet what that is." He proclaimed.

"You do not think the spirits led you to me to be with you? Wild Flower pleaded.

"I don't know, Wild Flower, I don't know." Angel replied, "That is why I must go. I must see what the spirits want me to do."

"Then I will plead with the spirits to bring you back to me" Wild Flower cried. As Angel got up on the horse.

This trip would be much faster. Angel had a horse, and the difference in the path he had to go would get him back to the town in a day and a half. He decided to camp by a pond that night. He had time to hunt up a rabbit, and he could cook rabbit better than most of the things he cooked, at least he thought so. He looked up into the sky after he had eaten and prepared for sleep. Angel was troubled he wasn't sure what lay ahead, but he knew, he could only be where he was. He smiled and pondered over the brave that kept showing up. He had not been around for a while. Of course Angel had not been around for a while either. His mind went to Heidi and if she would be waiting for him when he saw her. And back to Wild Flower and if he really wanted her for his squaw. His mind continued to question himself as he dozed off.

Angel woke to the smell of food cooking. He looked toward the fire. The brave was sitting cooking something in the fire.

"Ready to begin a new day?" The brave asked.

"Who are you/" Angel demanded.

Who do you want me to be?" The brave answered. Angel looked in the sky.

"Don't you know who you are?" Angel chided.

"Oh, I am a lot of things to a lot of people." The brave claimed, as he offered Angel some food.

Angel took the food and began to eat. And you are a lot of things to a lot of people. Who you are depends on where you are. When you are with your tribe you are a champion, when you are with others you are a guardian, and to yet others you are a burden, or an enemy."

"How can I be an enemy to people that don't even know who I am?" Angel wondered.

The brave answered, "The best answer is that you look different. Add to that you were raised a different way, and have different habits, different style, different language. Some are afraid of differences. Some just hate different ways of seeing things. And, there are some who know you are wasting time and effort by some of the things you do and know you won't hear when they try to show you a better way. There are many reasons to dislike a person who is different."

Angel looked at the brave, and said, "You still have not told me who you are."

The brave nodded and said, "With all of the questions in your head right now, who I am is not as important as who you are, or what you will do with what you know. You think your trial is over but you have much to learn and much to overcome, and much to survive."

"I have proven my bravery, my hunting skills, and my survival skills, "Angel pointed out, "What more must I prove?"

"Now you are trying to decide which path you will take, and how you decide will determine who you will become. No matter which path you walk there will be trouble, and there will be joys.. But you must decide. And you must live with the decisions you make. You already know that you are accepted and wanted by your tribe, and you know that if you decide to go to the other tribe, there will be some who will try to kill you just for making that decision. You know you will learn much more with the new tribe, and you will have an easier life, but some of your own kind will try to kill you for that decision.

Angel grimaced and yelled, "You are not making my decision any easier."

"Oh, but I am." the brave corrected, "Because you know you will do what your heart tells you to do.

You already made your decision, that is why you are here. That is why you are going back to the town."

Angel rose and prepared for the rest of this journey. "I guess you are right about that. I have decided to see what waits for me at the town. But I can still change my mind, I have not committed myself to anyone yet."

The brave stood and began walking away, "Yes, you can still change, that is always a choice you can make."

Angel climbed onto his horse and started toward the town.

As he approached Angel noticed the wall had been finished. He would have to go to the gate to get in. He hoped he had not been forgotten by the new tribe. He felt a fear again. He was after all an indian. And indians seemed to worry these people. The gate he chose was on the west side, where the headquarters was. He made sure he would not look like an attacker. This was not how he intended to die. The guard on duty saw Angel approaching and called, "who are you, friend or foe?"

"I am Angel. He replied, I am a friend of Major Matt."

The guard watched as Angel came nearer and shouted, "Angel, where have you been! We haven't seen you for a month seems like. Come on in. Hey Sarge! The Angel is back!"

Several people came to see Angel come in, and they seemed happy to see him.

"I know of one little girl that is gonna want to see you fer sure." The sergeant said as he shook Angel's hand. She's been moanin and groanin since you left."

Angel walked toward the houses. He had not taken twenty steps when he heard a scream.

"ANGEL! You're back!" Heidi yelled as she ran to him. She opened her arms and hugged him.

"Git yer hands off that lady!" a voice yelled. "Don't you put your stinkin paws on her."

Heidi turned toward the voice and shouted, "Hey I'm the one with my paw all over him you ain't got eyes."

A young man stepped up to Angel and pushed him back and stated, "I don't think you're man enough to have a white girl injun. And I think I'm gonna teach you how little of a man you are."

Angel stood still and looked at the crowd around them. What should he do now he wondered.

The young man kept prodding, "What's the matter injun? You got nuthin to say, or maybe you just can't talk. "

The sergeant stepped between the two that's enough. We don't need any fighting here boys. Then the young man made a mistake. He grabbed Heidi and started to push her away from Angel. Angel reached out and grabbed the boy by his collar and threw him to the ground.

"You keep hands off Heidi. She come to me. She not come to you. I not want to fight,. but I not lose."

The sergeant brought two privates over to keep the two apart. Angel had no intention of doing more than he'd already done. He just wanted this kid to go away. Toby, the young man wanted all injuns dead. But for now, there would be peace. And for now Heidi wanted Angel to stay with her.

They walked back to Heidi's house. Audrey, and Mathew smiled and said hello to him and he returned the greeting. Mrs. Krause was happy he had returned too.

Angel noticed as they walked that there was a wagon with men in it, and they had darker skin than he had. They were in a cage. Angel didn't understand.

"Why men in wagon?" Angel questioned.

Heidi answered, "those are slaves. They belong to the man at the end of the wagon.

Angel looked for the man and saw another black man leaning against the wagon. Angel wondered about it, but, he had more to think about right now. For now the reunion was the important thing.

Knowing that Heidi still liked him gave Angel a lift he had not felt in a very long time. He left welcomed among these people. And they showed their happiness much more than his people did.

Chapter
FOURTEEN

Mrs. Krause lit the candle as the evening drew on toward night. She had been watching her daughter and Angel enjoying each other's company. Angel was quite uncomfortable almost pushing Heidi away at times as she tried to mash herself against him. And though he tried to be mannerly about the situation, Mrs Krause could see the desire in his eyes. She remembered how she had looked at Otto, and how he had looked at her.

"Heidi." She said, "I am getting tired, I will go to sleep soon. But I vish to talk with you both first."

At first Angel thought he had done something wrong from the tone of Mrs. Krause voice. But Heidi almost ignored her mother, until Angel settled her down.

"I see how you are together. She began, "I am afraid for you. I know of what happened earlier vhen you met. This vill not be the only time someone vill not vant to see the two of you together. For a white girl to be vis a dark skinned indian, this vill bring trouble."

"I don't care momma, I love him!" Heidi blurted out. Angel was surprised that Heidi showed so much anger towards her mother, but stayed silent, he could see Mrs. Krause was not finished.

"I know you do sweetheart, I can see the same look in your eye as I had for my Otto. I know how you feel, and I do not mind that the two of you care so much for each other. But, you must be avare of vhat others think of it. There are many who cannot stand the idea."

Angel looked at Heidi, and back at Mrs. Krause, and said, "I see anger you speak of Mrs. Krause, I have been told skins don't go together, but I feel much for Heidi."

"I know Angel," Mrs. Krause continued, "I can see in your eyes the look of love. I feel fear for you though. You are very young, There vill be enough problems in normal living, you u vill have many more if you come together. And it vill never end."

Heidi frowned, "Why can't you be happy for us momma? We will not be treated too badly once people understand we love each other.

"No, "Angel responded, "Your mother right. There be many who will hate both for being together.

Many who were friends, will be enemies, and many will see only skin, and not heart. This I see."

Heidi began to sob, "You don't want me Angel?' She groaned.

Angel looked in Heidi's eyes and said softly, "I not say I not want you Heidi. I say many of your skin, and of my skin will hate if we stay together. I not wanted in many places in this town, and you not wanted by many in my tribe. We must fight the fight all fight to live, and we must fight the hate of those that will hate our skins."

Mrs. Krause rose and began to go to the room in the back of the house.

"I think Angel knows what I am trying to say, I hope you can get my daughter to understand too."

As soon as Mrs. Krause closed the door, Heidi went to Angel's lap. Angel was stunned that this girl was moving so quickly. The girls he had watched grow up always waited for the brave to come to them.

They had always acted shy, even the ones he knew wanted those men, were always quite demure.

Heidi had no trouble letting Angel know how she felt, and didn't care who knew, or what they thought of it.

She bent to his face and kissed him. Angel pulled her to him and they embraced. Angel was the first to pull away. He stared at the girl he was holding. He was amazed at how beautiful this girl was, and she wanted him. And she wanted him now! She pressed herself against him in total abandon.

Angel wasn't sure how to react to how this girl was acting. And his own desire was building.

Angel let his hand slip down Heidi's back. Suddenly, she jumped away from Angel.

"What are you doing?" she demanded.

"I do what you do." Angel countered, "You come to me, I hold you, what Angel do wrong?"

"You need to keep your hands away from, parts of me. "She stammered.

Angel broke out in laughter. Heidi started to get mad. Angel stood up. And turned toward the door.

"Angel not stay if he upsets Heidi" He said, and began to walk away.

"No!" Heidi gasped, and ran around Angel to get to the door. "That's not what you are

suppose to do."

She said. "You are suppose to.

Angel put both arms around Heidi and pulled her to him, "I not suppose to, I Angel, I do what Angel do." And he kissed her. She acted angry, like she would push him away, but her arms went around Angels neck. She knew she lost control, and she didn't care. She would play by his rules.

Angel knew he could have Heidi now, but he didn't feel right. He stayed with Heidi for a long time that night, but he felt closed in knowing that her mother was only a door away. He stared at her again before he left and stated, "You be Angel's squaw soon, I be back."

Heidi wasn't sure what had happened. She had offered herself to him. And he did not take what she offered. She thought maybe it was just an indian thing. He wasn't angry. He said he would be back.

And she knew what a squaw was, maybe there was a ceremony or something he had to do. Whatever it was, she wished he had not left her yet. It would take time to get to sleep now. She would be up for a long time.

Angel found a place to sleep against the wall. He would sleep soon. He was exhausted. He did consider all that had happened that night. He was pleased with himself. She had played a game, and he won. He wasn't sure what game she was playing, but he knew she did not want him to stop. She did not care if others knew they would be together. In his tribe the whole tribe would know. It was important that no other brave would try to take a brave's squaw. And, from what he saw of the major and Audrey, and Otto and Mrs. Krause, they wanted everybody to know too, and for the same reason.

Angel left the town early. He headed into the forest to find a place to build. He had watched his father gather branches and frame a hut. He had borrowed an ax and a saw for his hut. This would be a better hut than his father made, he thought, better tools better hut. He looked over his work and decided it would stand anything but nature's winds, and a buffalo stampede, Another memory of his father.

Heidi didn't understand at all. She had waited all day for Angel to return. She thought he should have been around for breakfast. Now he missed lunch, and it was almost supper time. Her mother watched and tried to understand. She had no idea what had happened last night, but she suspected one of the two had said or done something wrong. Angel had gone, and Heidi was acting like her world had just crumbled. Perhaps he had used her and left, but, she showed no anger, or remorse. She had tried to talk to Heidi about it, but Heidi would only say, "He said he'd be back momma."

Angel came walking in just as Mrs. Krause was ready to serve up her, now famous stew.

Everyone who had tried it thought it was "The best stew they had ever tasted." She had even been asked if she would like to start a kitchen and sell her stew. That sounded like a good idea considering she didn't have Otto to support her or Heidi. vell, I sure am glad you came back Angel.

"Where Heidi?" he asked.

"She's inside sulking at the moment." Mrs. Krause answered.

Angel put his hand on Mrs. Krause shoulder and said, "Heidi wants Angel and Angel wants Heidi, you are mother of Heidi, what you think?"

Mrs. Krause was taken aback. She hadn't been sure what to say, she had not thought she would be asked, certainly Heidi didn't ask.

"Angel, I don't think I could keep that girl avay from you if I didn't like you, but, I do like you, you are a very good man. I just hope you are not asking for trouble from the bigots around here." She answered.

Angel nodded, "There will be trouble Mrs. Krause. I not want trouble, but I know trouble will come."

Mrs. Krause giggled and said, "Vell, if you are going to have my daughter, you better start calling me momma!"

"Angel!" Heidi cried, "You're back!" as he and Momma came into the house. The three sat down to a great meal. There was not much conversation this evening. Angel ate like he hadn't eaten all day. After the meal was over, Angel rose from the table and said.

"Heidi, I will take you to be my squaw this night." He watched the reactions from both. Heidi was elated, Momma smiled.

"You must come with me now." He commanded, looking at Heidi.

Heidi rose from her chair, looked back at Momma and said, "I love you momma, but I love Angel too. I have to go." and she walked to Angel's side.

Momma smiled, as tear welled up in her eyes, "This isn't how I expected you to go Heidi. Angel, you vill not keep her avay long, vill you?"

Angel smiled, "We come back Momma, soon we come back.

Chapter
FIFTEEN

It had been three days since Angel and Heidi left. Mrs. Krause was lonely. She had set up a kitchen of sorts, feeding some soldiers and the slaves in the cages. She was being paid well. The idea of starting a business was paying off. She missed Heidi, and Otto, she had not been alone for 16 years.

It was nearly noon when the drums began to sound. It was scary at first, but a nice steady beat.

Most of the towns people were confused by it. The soldiers were scurrying around taking up positions around the wall. Rumors of an imminent indian attack flew around the town. It seemed like the drums would sound for about five minutes, then it would be quiet for a few minutes, then the drums would start again.

It had been about an hour since the pounding of the drums began, when Heidi made it to the town. She saw her mother stoking the fire pit to keep the fire going.

"I'm home Momma!" she yelled.

Mrs. Krause looked up from her work, dropped her stick, and ran to her daughter.

"Oh meine kinder is home" She gushed. Looking passed her daughter, she asked, "And vhere is Angel?"

"He said he had to go to a meeting, "Heidi answered. "I guess that's what the drums are about. Angel said the tribes were getting together for a meeting, something about this time of the year."

Momma looked at her little girl. She had the glow of a new bride, but she needed a bath Momma thought, and some clean clothes.

Suddenly, there was a new set of drums, from a different direction, with a different beat. And the first drums answered the new beat. A man came rushing through the camp. He stopped when he got to Mrs. Krause.

"Why ain't you two in your houses! "He yelled, "We could be attacked any minute!"

Heidi smiled at the man and said, "Nobody is going to attack us, at least not now."

The man couldn't understand why these ladies weren't scared. About that time the Major walked over from his house, after hearing the yelling.

"Everything okay over here Helga? "He asked. "aren't you going to go inside for cover."

Heidi looked puzzled. "Why do we need cover, there is no threat that I can see."

Matt knew the Krause' well enough now to realize they knew something he didn't know. And he knew Heidi had been gone with Angel for three days. He asked.

"Okay, Heidi, what are those drums all about?"

The man that had been rushing up to the ladies was awe struck. An army major was asking a girl for information. His jaw dropped. He had to see what this girl would say.

Heidi was pleased that she was being given credit. It was unusual enough for a man tothink a woman knew anything about customs of the natives, but to ask a woman for advice was unheard of.

"Angel said," She began, "That those drums are calling the tribes together. It is some sort of a reunion. This time of the year the tribes meet for a ceremony of some kind."

Another set of drums began to sound, and the first set responded, then the second set reported.

The second set had moved closer to the first set.

The major looked at Heidi, "This is only a reunion?"

Heidi crinkled her nose, "That's what Angel told me."

The Major smiled, "If Angel said it, I guess it's true. I better tell the Colonel. Have a wonderful day ladies." He said as he headed toward the Colonel's office.

The man stood there amazed at what he had witnessed. He finally turned around and started walking back to his wagon, muttering as he went.

Angel wanted to know how the counsel of the tribes were thinking. He knew things were changing. He knew there would be talk of destroying the pale skins. He knew many of the wise men of the counsel would not want war. He had to know how they would decide to cope with the new world that was coming to their land. The tribes came together at this time of year because they were closer now than they would be until the cold times. There were tribes that stayed in the area all year long, and tribes like Angel's that followed the trails to the north in the warm times, and south in the cold times.

The elders of his tribe had said that they follow the sun. Angel had wondered about that since the sun moved east to west. He had asked his father why the elder didn't know which way the sun went. His father had told him.

"The sun does move east to west my son, but as the days go by the sun gets higher in the sky, until the warm times are over, then it gets lower in the sky until the cold times are over. We do follow the sun from warm to cold and back."

Angel had paid attention after that and realized that his father, and the elders were right. It became colder as the sun leaned to the south, and warmer as the sun leaned north. The sun would be at it's northern peak in only a few days. In two or three moons the southern migration would begin.

Angel remembered the time the tribe had remained with a tribe that stayed all year. It had been so cold and the rain turned white. The hunting was miserable. Angel never wanted to stay through the cold times again.

When Angel arrived at the meeting grounds, a large meadow by a brook, he saw two of the old chiefs of the tribes that stayed all year, and one of the renegade tribe chiefs already there. They were speaking only of the intruding pale skins and how they were destroying the land, and killing their people.

"These savages are killing whole tribes. "The renegade was saying, "Even the children are not spared. They have no respect for the land, or the families that have kept the land for all of our generations. They must be stopped! And the only way to stop them is to kill them."

One of the other chiefs replied, "Their number is growing in our land too. The more we kill, the more that come over the mountains. I have journeyed to the east of the mountains to see where they come from. They are many. If we are to stop them we must first keep them from traveling through the mountains."

As Angel came nearer the renegade chief looked at him and said.

"Little Bear, have you seen the horrors the pale skins do?"

Angel brightened a little, "I have seen." He answered.

"Where is Buffalo Hunter, your father. I have not seen him yet." the chief said.

Angel grimaced and said, "My father is dead, as is most of my tribe. Only the old and very young remain. I am a brave now. Gray Wolf calls me Avenging Spirit."

"Will Gray Wolf come, Avenging Spirit, or did he send you as the new chief.?" The chief demanded.

"I expect Gray Wolf to come." Angel offered, and began to tell the story of the raid on his tribe. The chiefs listened.

One of the chiefs after listening assuming Avenging Spirit to be angry said.

"So, now you will join the fight against the pale skins."

Angel answered without hesitation.

"My father told me once that there are always good and bad people in every tribe. And he was right."

Angel looked around at the men listening, that was growing. He counted ten now.

"I have watched these people build a village in one moon that is stronger and more secure than what we can build. They use tools that are faster and better than ours. And they have weapons that kill more braves faster than I have ever seen. I watched as Red Eagle's tribe attacked their village and were killed before they came close enough to use their spears."

Angel paused and noticed the crowd around him was still growing.

"I have found that there are many among the pale skins that have hate for our people, but many would live beside us too. If we could learn of the good things they can bring to our people, the tools, the knowledge of how to build it could be a very good thing. We would not work as hard. And, if we do not learn of their ways, we have no chance of killing them, or getting them out of our land."

"But how do you live with killers?" a voice rang out.

Angel thought for a minute, and said, "We live with killers in our own tribes. Wailing coyote, and Running Deer, and Crooked Bow were killers, Red Eagle and his tribe were killers. We lived with them until they were killed. It can be no different with the pale skins. If we find a killer, he must die."

"You speak with the tongue of youth." The voice stated. The audience turned to Chief Brown Feather. "It is so much easier to surrender to the pale skins, and become their slaves, but it is not right that a proud Cherokee people should become slaves to the pale skins. I will die before I give up our land or the ways of our fathers to be a slave to the pale skins."

The drums had ceased by now and the tribes continued to argue over the pale skins. Angel was taken by how many had come to hear him speak. He had always been counted with the children before. The elders ignored the children when addressing the problems of the tribes. Now he had gained the rank of, not just a brave, but, one who had knowledge. That did not usually come to one as young as Angel. The ceremony of the meeting would begin soon. Angel wondered where he would be placed in the ceremony.

Gray Wolf came over to Angel, glad to see he had made it.

"Avenging Spirit," He said, "You must take the seat of your father now. You will be the voice of our tribe."

Angel nodded, "I hope I will show the wisdom of my father in this counsel, Gray Wolf."

"Avenging Spirit!" Wild Flower called, "You are here! I have missed you. I hoped you would come."

Angel cringed, and said, "It is good that we have come together at this time. There are many things that have happened to us both to discuss."

For three days the counsel met and argued over the pale skins, and whether they would be at war or not. As one would get up and try to compel the tribes to attack the pale skins, another would warn of the dangers of a war. Then all went silent as Bear Claw rose to address the counsel. Bear Claw was known as one who had been vanquished from east of the mountains, he had once lived on the shores of the great sea. He had lived where the pale skins were coming from. He looked around the tribes and began, "My friends, I have seen how the pale skins began settling in our land. And I have seen some of our people killed, some because of the pale skins hate, and some because of our people's hate. I have seen agreements that both our people and the pale skins kept, and agreements both have broken.

We were told if we moved to your land we would live well, and they would live well. Now, they are moving here to your land. And they will say if we move again, we will be safe again. But, they already are moving past this land even farther. I have spoken with braves that have come from the great river toward the setting sun. They tell of more pale skins there, who travel the river and are moving every way from there. If we go to war, we will need many tribes to kill all of the pale skins.

And many of our own people will die."

Angel rose, "elders of the tribes hear me," He began, "My father told me to hunt buffalo is dangerous. You should not try to kill more than one at a time, and be sure you are not in front of them if they stampede, they will kill you. We are talking about killing a whole herd of buffalo with only one knife. And when this herd is upset it stampedes over all things in it's way. Be very careful if you want to war with these people. I do not want to make war with them."

Chief Brown Feather, rose and spoke, "You sound as if you have lived with these pale skins, Avenging Spirit."

"I have." Angel responded, "I have learned to speak their tongue, and understand their words. They can be nice people, or a vicious enemy. They have many men who practice only how to kill. Those who practice turning skins into clothing become very good at making clothing. The more you practice, the better you get. These men have practiced war, they are very good at it Chief Brown Feather spat toward Angel, and growled, "So you have already surrendered and become a slave."

"I am a slave to no man! "Angel shouted, "I have proven myself to both the pale skins and our people. And I have been accepted as an avenging spirit to both people. And I have done it with honor. I did not have to ask to come to this counsel. I came to hear my people and try to help make our lives better, and easier. You came to make war. If you make war with these pale skins you will die. If you learn their ways, you can get rid of the bad ones without war."

The last night celebration was uneasy. Several tribes left vowing to kill the pale skins, and those that stayed worried for their future. Gray Wolf decided it would be better to begin their southern journey now.

"waiting could cost the lives of those in my care, and I have no braves to protect us." He moaned.

Angel promised to see them all again, but vowed to try to bring both peoples together.

Chapter
SIXTEEN

ngel was not sure what he should do. If he told the soldiers of the tribes that would attack he would be undermining his people, but if he didn't tell, he endangered his and his squaw's lives, along with many in the town. He felt obligated to both. But the pale skins weren't trying hurt anyone. It was the tribes that would be led by Brown Feather that intended to kill.

He decided to stop by his hut. As he approached he saw a figure by the fire pit. He knew who it was.

"So, now you are more confused than ever." The Brave started, as he turned to look at Angel.

"You knew it was me?" Angel stammered.

"Who else would it be?" The brave casually stated.

"Yes," Angel laughed," and who else would you be. What are we going to talk about today?"

The brave smiled, "How about women." He said, "You never told Wild Flower about Heidi."

Angel was puzzled, "You weren't there, how would you know what or who I talked to?" He demanded.

"That is not the problem here." The brave noted, "We are talking about how you treated the girl that was to become your squaw."

"I had no time for that, I was called to be in the counsel." Angel countered.

The brave was not to be side tracked, "That is an excuse Angel. You made sure you had no time just so you would not have to tell her."

Angel knew he was trapped. "How can I tell one I grew up with that the dreams we shared have been ruined by one I only knew for a short time? He stammered.

"Or, "the brave suggested, "Perhaps if you find that Heidi is not right for you, you can go back to Wild Flower."

Angel deflected, "Well, no one witnessed a ceremony. No chief, or mother, or pale skin to see what happened."

"But the spirits know Angel, "the brave said, "And they will hold you to your words to Heidi, and no words to Wild Flower. In fact, the spirits are drawing her here now." And the brave left.

"Drawing her here? Which one are they drawing? Why are you leaving now?" Angel shouted.

"You said we had to talk Avenging spirit." Wild Flower said as she came into Angel's camp.

"You followed me?" Angel gasped.

"We were promised to each other Avenging Spirit." She answered, "Where should I go?"

Angel tried to think. He was trapped. There was only one way out, the truth.

"Wild Flower, I did not talk to you because I was afraid." Angel said, "We were told long ago that the journey to maturity held many disappointments. That we can't always keep the promises of our youth."

"Then, it is true, "Wild Flower exclaimed, "You have taken the pale skin woman." She reached over and traced the crease on the side of Angel's head.

Angel nodded and said, "It seemed more like she took me."

Wild Flower walked in circles for several minutes. She remembered her mother telling her that when a brave came back from his trial it could change him. That this would not be the first time a brave had a change of heart. But there were no more men of the right age in their tribe now.

Angel considered her situation, and offered, "I wish I could offer you more, but I did make a commitment. If I," Wild Flower cut him off, "No! Little Bear, all I want to know, right now, is if you still have feelings for me."

Angel smiled, and said, "Yes, Wild Flower. I feel much for you. That is why I was ashamed to tell you."

Wild Flower walked away from the camp site. Angel was alone. He thought about his feelings for Heidi, and his feelings for Wild Flower. He knew Wild Flower, they grew up together.

Heidi he did not know well, but she brought out his lust. She made him want her. And she did not wait for him to show what he wanted. She made sure he knew what she wanted. He did not have to ask and hope she would be willing, she was not only willing, she was demanding.

It wasn't long before Angel remembered He should be thinking about war. He knew the odds were against his people. He also knew there were enough pale skins who would use any excuse to exterminate as many indians as they could. He also knew that many of his people felt the same about the pale skins. He started back to the town.

He stopped at the edge of the forest, to see if it was safe. He looked at the wall, and the guards along the wall. One was looking in his direction. Angel watched as the soldier brought his rifle to his shoulder. Angel dodged behind a tree. The rifle sounded and the bullet bit the tree Angel was behind.

Other soldiers came to see what had happened.

"There's a injun in them trees yonder. "The shooter yelled.

"I am Angel." Angel yelled. "I am Angel." He peeked around the tree and saw three other rifles pointed in his direction. He realized these soldiers didn't know him. He called out.

"I call for Major Matt, and Mrs. Krause."

He looked again. The rifles had not moved. There was some talking going on, and one soldier left the others. He heard a familiar voice, "Who goes there?" It was the Colonel's voice.

"I am Angel. "He repeated.

"At ease men. "the Colonel commanded, "Come on in Angel." he called.

Angel came to the front gate where the Colonel met him.

"So, what were all of those drums about Angel?" The colonel asked.

Angel felt good that he was considered a source for information, but was not sure how much information he should give.

"We have meeting every warm season, "He stated, "Decide what to do to keep tribes at peace."

"So this is just a regular meeting." The colonel stated.

"Talk about pale skins taking land," Angel confessed. "Talk of war."

The colonel became very serious. "They are talking of war?"

Angel put up his hand, "many talk of war, many talk of peace. Some say war only way to get rid of bad pale skins. Angel say, many good pale skins, make no trouble. Many kill tribes only to kill tribes."

The colonel thought for a minute, and said, "That is a problem isn't it. Any idea when that could come?"

"Chiefs not talk of when or how war comes, only that it comes. Pale skins come into land, not try to learn of tribal ways, only kill and take land. Destroy hunting grounds, destroy camp grounds. "Angel pointed out. "How tribes see good, when all is bad. Angel come back to be with town, soldiers shoot Angel. Where is good, Colonel?"

The colonel looked at the ground. "I guess it does look that way from the indian side doesn't it."

Angel wasn't done, "Angel only friend for saving Major, And Krause', if not, Angel enemy too. How we make peace if all are enemy." Angel finished, and went toward Heidi's house. The colonel nodded and went to his headquarters.

Chapter
SEVENTEEN

Three days had passed since the counsel had met. Angel had taken Heidi back to their hut. All seemed to be going well, until, Heidi looked at Angel and said.

"I don't want to live out here in the woods any more, Angel. I want to live in town."

Angel didn't know what to do, so he said.

"We have no home in the town, where we live?"

"We have no home here either, "She shot back, "This is not a home. What will we do when the winter comes. We will freeze."

"We move to warm place in cold." Angel commanded.

Heidi was adamant. "I won't leave my mother to go wandering around the countryside. We need to build a house, in town!" she demanded.

"Angel not builder of house, Angel build hut, like father build hut." Angel commanded.

Heidi got mad. "Then I will live in my mother's house, you can stay in your hut." She shouted, and started back to town.

Angel followed wondering what he did wrong. As they arrived a soldier was running from the east side of the town.

"Sergeant, "He shouted.

"What is it private?" the sergeant demanded.

The private caught his breath, and reported, "Sergeant, a hunting party of five went to find food a while ago. Some injuns brought their bodies and tossed em out of the woods just a few minutes ago."

The sergeant nodded, "I'll tell the Colonel, private, carry on."

"Yes, sergeant." the private said, and headed back to his post. The sergeant rushed to the colonel's office.

Heidi continued to her mother's house. Angel stopped and watched the people who heard the private start talking and moving from one to another. This was not good Angel thought. When he finally got to the house he went in and Heidi began to yell.

"Get away from me! I am not gonna live in a forest with no walls! Get out of this house! I never should have let you get near me! I don't want to see you again!"

Angel was in shock. Mrs. Krause went to Angel.

"I guess you had better leave Angel." She said, "She seems pretty upset."

Angel left, the house, and the town. It appeared to him that their relationship was over. He found his way back to the hut. He tried to figure out what had just happened. He plodded around his campsite muttering to himself.

"This a perfectly good hut." he muttered. "Why does the pale skin woman expect Angel to live like pale skin, she knew I was not a pale skin when she came to me. What is wrong with pale skins? I like Angel's hut."

"I think it's a wonderful hut, "Wild Flower interrupted.

Angel froze. This was the first time anyone had been able to sneak up on him. Even as a child no one could surprise him. And surprise him she did.

"Why are you here?" Angel demanded.

Wild Flower giggled, "Because I knew you would need me."

Angel wasn't ready to calm down. He demanded, "Why do I need you?"

Wild Flower was enjoying the moment, and said, "The pale skins don't do well in the forest do they?"

"How long have you been watching me?" Angel growled.

Wild Flower sighed and said, "I never went far away. I knew it wouldn't work out. It could not work, she cannot live like you do, for long, and you cannot live like her people do." wild Flower came to Angel, and touched his shoulder.

"She is very pretty, she is also not a squaw. She is still a girl. She has not grown up yet."

Angel considered her words. Wild Flower went on, "She did not try to clean your hut. She did not make food for her brave. She did not help with the work. And, if she did not like the hut, why did she not fix it so she did like it, like a good squaw."

Angel began to calm down. He pondered all that had happened. He looked into Wild Flower's smiling face.

"But, I took her as my squaw. I can't take it back. Am I just to forget I had her?" Angel wondered.

Wild Flower frowned, "No. You can't just take it back Little Bear, and she may still come back to you.

How will you act if she does? Will you take her back in?"

"I don't know." He admitted, "I did not think she would come back. She told me not to come back. Why would she come back?"

"Why did she go?" Wild Flower asked, "If she left because of the hut only, then why would she come back to it? And if there were more reasons, she might come back, but, would she tell you why?"

Angel grew suspicious. "Why do you tell me these things?"

"Because I want to be your squaw." Wild Flower said, as she drew closer to him, "I want my Little Bear, back. I can't have you if you are still with her."

"But if you know you can't have me until she is gone, why are you acting like you are my squaw?"

Angel demanded.

Wild Flower smiled, and said, "You said she got you because she took you. I will let you know that when you are ready to let her go, I will take you. I will stay with you and comfort you until she comes back, or you want me."

Angel frowned, "What if I don't want you to stay around."

Wild Flower's smile grew, "Then I will go back to my camp until you do, Little Bear. I know it will take time, I know you can't make promises until you know what she will do. I can wait here as well as I can wait with the tribe. I made a promise to you once that I would stay by your side always I never forgot, and I never changed my mind. Even though I may never get you I will treat you like you are my Little Bear."

Angel laughed, "You don't see me as a brave yet?"

"Not as long as you act like you are not a brave, besides, I love Little Bear, and I will probably always think of you as the boy I grew up with. And, I am not sure I like the idea of being the squaw of 'Avenging Spirit".

Angel laughed again, "I tried very hard to out grow Little Bear, and you want to keep calling me by it. You do know me well my Wild Flower."

Wild Flower pressed against Angel. She looked into his eyes and whispered, One day I will know you better."

Angel kissed her. Wild flower drew back in surprise. Her eyes widened.

"Why did you do that?" She stammered.

"This is a thing I learned from the pale skins, and I like it." he laughed.

Wild Flower moved her lips around wondering how she should react to this new feeling. Angel kissed her again. This time she pushed her lips back at him trying to imitate his moves. As she backed away again she wondered.

"Is this what friends do, or what a brave and his squaw do?"

"I only know Heidi did it to me. I have seen no other pale skins do it." Angel responded.

Wild Flower brightened up more and leaned into Angel and kissed him back.

"It does feel good. "she said, "I think it is more for lovers than what we are now though."

For three days the two friends hunted played and enjoyed each other. Wild Flower slept behind Angel at night hoping one day he would decide to take her and leave the other girl behind, but she was true to her word. She would not act like a squaw until he decided to give up on the pale skin.

The sun was high in the sky when Angel heard the voice.

"Angel!, Angel!"

Angel went to find who was calling. He recognized the voice, but wasn't sure who it was right away.

Then he heard the call again, "Angel!, Angel!"

It was the major.

"I am here." Angel yelled.

The major found Angel's camp. Wild Flower had vanished into the forest.

"Angel, we need you in town. Indians have been raiding our hunting parties. The colonel sent me to get you, to find out how to stop these attacks." The major said.

"How you find Angel?" Angel demanded.

The major smiled a little and answered, "The colonel had me go and ask Heidi where to go."

Angel looked at the major, and asked "what can Angel do? Me no fight whole tribe."

"No you couldn't." The major responded, "But, you can talk to them. You could ask what they want in order to make peace with the town."

Angel smiled and said, "you go to other land. They make peace."

The major smiled back and pleaded, "Please come back with me Angel. You saved us before please be our angel again."

Angel thought for a moment, got up and walked to the major.

"Okay, I go."

Chapter

Eighteen

Angel walked into the colonel's office.

"Angel, let me get right to the point," the colonel began, "You made a lot of sense the other day. Our people have come into this land without asking permission, and have not really tried to learn about the society we have disrupted."

Angel nodded.

"You know these people." The colonel continued, "You have learned of our people, and our language."

Angel did not understand, "What language?" he inserted.

"You know, our words." the colonel explained.

Angel nodded.

The colonel continued, "You can talk to your people and ours. Angel, I am ready to pay you to go to the indians that are attacking us and talk about how we can live together in this land. I will even give you rank and benefits if we can just stop the killing."

Angel considered the colonel's proposition. "What is rank? What is benefits?" He questioned.

The colonel had to think of how to answer that question.

"You have chiefs, and braves, we have privates, and sergeants, and I am a colonel, those are ranks, benefits are extra incentives, ah, like a house to live in."

"Angel get house, not have to build?" Angel asked, more than a little shocked.

"There are a couple of houses that are no longer being used." The colonel admitted, "two families decided to move on to the west."

"But, Angel go to warm country soon, not like cold." Angel protested.

The colonel smiled, "These houses will be much warmer than the huts you have lived in."

Angel thought about the offer, "What if Angel not get chiefs to talk peace? Can talk, cannot make chiefs make peace. They say, pale skins leave, then comes peace."

The colonel became very serious, "Listen Angel, I was sent here to establish, ah, ah, make a town, and a military post in this area. Once I decided on this spot, I now must defend the town. That means I must either find a way to make peace with your people or I must kill those who will not make peace. I would much rather make peace than to kill, or be killed. The raiding parties that have been killing our hunting parties are causing a lot of pain. And many of the town's people are demanding I stop the killing. If we cannot make peace, I will be forced to send out soldiers to kill any that MAY be part of the raiding parties. Many will die, many that are killing our people, and many who are not. I am asking you to help me to not kill."

Angel considered all he heard the colonel say. He thought about Brown Feather and how hard it might be to convince him to make peace with the pale skins. The colonel added.

"Angel, if things get too bad, I will have to bring more soldiers, and kill many more people."

"Angel will try." Angel said. "Angel does not like killing.

As Angel walked out of the headquarters he thought about what to say. The colonel had offered an escort of soldiers to go with him to bargain with the tribes, but Angel thought that would hurt talks more than help. He looked over to the lake and watched the women working and children playing. He saw Heidi. He wondered what to do about her. Then he saw a boy she was with, and she was treating the boy the same way she had treated him. Mrs. Krause was cooking, as usual. Angel paused.

"It is good day." He said, to Mrs. Krause.

She smiled, and said, "Yes, it is a very good day today. How are you doing Angel?"

Angel good, "He replied, "How Heidi? He asked, hoping for information.

Mrs. Krause frowned, "It appears she has started something vith Jeffrey, I think. "She hoped she wasn't hurting Angel, but she continued, "It seems like you vere only a phase she vas going through."

Angel did not understand phase' but knew Heidi had moved on and left him behind. He wasn't sure how he felt about that but, he would have to live. He had enjoyed his time with her. But, Wild Flower would always be there he thought.

He did a lot of thinking on his way to meet Brown Feather. He thought of how Wild Flower would act when she found that Heidi was no longer a problem. He thought of what it might be like to live in a house in the cold times. And he thought of what he should say when he got to Brown Feather's tribe.

Angel heard the rustle of human activity. He knew he was close to the tribe's area. He called out to the tribe. "I have come to speak with Brown Feather."

There was a pause as he continued toward the tribe.

"Who are you?"

"I am Avenging Spirit." He responded.

As Angel walked into the camp, he was directed to Brown Feather's tent.

"And, what brings Avenging Spirit to Brown Feather's camp?" Brown Feather began.

Angel smiled, "I have come to try to make peace in the land." He offered.

Brown Feather laughed, "You, the man who showed us how to attack the pale skins, wants to talk of peace in the land. That is funny Avenging Spirit."

Angel was confused, "I showed you? "He asked.

"It was your story of hunting buffalo spoke of how to fight these people." Brown Feather told him.

Angel nodded, and said, "It has worked well then. The pale skins have asked me to come and ask for peace."

Brown Feather was strengthened and asked, "Why should we talk peace, why should we not get rid of the pale skins." Angel's face grew serious, and he began, "Brown Feather, hear me, the chief of the people in the town has talked to me. He said that his soldiers must defend this town. He does not want his people or ours to die. He knows many will die if the war continues. And he has said that more soldiers will come if there is not peace. He told me if we cannot find a way to make peace he will send many soldiers to kill you, and all of your tribe. He does not want to kill that many of our people. He is not ordering our people Brown Feather, he is begging to make peace."

Brown feather frowned, "This I hear from you, Avenging Spirit, you whose tribe was killed by these pale skins. You believe there will be peace."

"Those that killed my tribe were not of the town. I tracked those men and killed them myself. I do not know that there can be peace, but, I do know many more will die if there is no peace, than will die if we try to make peace. "Angel concluded.

The two talked for a long time. When Angel finally left he was smiling. He thought he had done well. Now he could give the colonel Brown Feather's conditions to make peace and he felt he would become an admired brave, by both people. And he surely had many stories, and would have many more to tell at the camp fires.

The sun was nearly down when Angel got near the town. As he walked, he heard the noise of a twig snapping. He looked in the direction and prepared to defend himself if needed.

"Little Bear, I have been waiting." Wild Flower announced.

"It seems more like you were following." Angel replied.

Wild Flower laughed, "I worried how long you would be gone." She said.

Angel brightened up, as he asked, "Wild Flower, would you like to live in a pale skins house? It has been offered to us. It would be warmer in the cold times."

Wild Flower had not considered living any where near the pale skins. She speculated, "I have never been in those houses, how would I know if I liked it?" Then it hit her, "You will live in the house with me? We will live together? What about Heidi?"

Angel grinned, "Heidi is with another man now. She will not come back."

Wild Flower frowned and commented, "Unless she has your child."

She stopped Angel and asked, "What is this angel they said when they called for you?"

Angel smiled, "Angel is the pale skin's word for protector."

"That is a good name Little Bear." she said," I like that you are Angel."

Angel laughed, "The pale skins call me protector, our people call me avenger, and for you I did both."

Wild Flower beamed as they got to the east gate of the town.

The colonel was anxious to hear what Angel had found out. He offered a chair and prepared to listen. Angel began, "Brown Feather will make peace with pale skins, but he wants to protect his people. He say, the wagon trains that come through must stay on trail. If braves find pale skin in forest they will die. He say none come out of town. I say,how do pale skins hunt if not out of town? He say we make area for town to hunt. We not know what area now. He say, if pale skin, or group of pale skins do harm to indian, tribe punish indian way. If indian do harm to pale skin, pale skin punish pale skin way."

The colonel pondered the offer and said, "I will take this under advisement. It sounds like a pretty fair agreement, but as to who punishes who, there may be some problems with that."

Angel spoke again, "Brown Feather say, he see you face to face to make peace. Angel only bring the words, the colonel in charge."

The colonel wondered about that, but realized it would be his word that would make it legal, so to speak. They talked for a while longer. As the colonel began to get up to leave angel asked another question, "When does Angel get house?"

The colonel laughed, and called in a captain, "Captain," He commanded, "Show our angel one of the empty houses in our town."

They left and Angel was brought to a house that had been abandoned for it's occupants to move on. It was a big house Angel thought. And he saw a fire pit inside. This may do well Angel thought.

Chapter

NINETEEN

"I am afraid, Little Bear." Wild Flower explained, "You have come to know these people, I do not know their words, I do not know their way, and they may hate."

"I see hate in all tribes." Angel replied, "I see love in all tribes. There will always be some who hate.

I did not know their words before, I learned, by listening to their words and how they used their words.

The same way I learned our words. You learned 'Angel', you know what it means, you can learn more.

You do not know them, but, they do not know you. You cannot know them without meeting them."

Wild Flower knew he would go. She knew she would go. She looked at the ground and grumbled, "I am not a brave, why must I go through the trial of a brave?"

"Because, "Angel gloated, "You want Angel."

Wild Flower turned away from Angel, and grimaced, and then giggled. She turned back to Angel and kissed him, and said.

"And I will have you. And, if you can learn their words, surely, I can learn their words."

The sound was crisp, someone, or something was approaching the hut. Angel came out to see what was coming while Wild Flower ran behind a tree. As the dark skinned man came into the open, and saw the camp, he threw his arms in the air.

"Please don't hurt me!" The man begged.

"Why hurt you?" Angel replied.

"They's gonna skin me alive if they catches me." He claimed as he tried to catch his breath.

"You do bad?" Angel asked.

"Only thing I done, "the man claimed, "Is I runned away and hid from ma owner. I hope I runned far enough ta git away. I won't be a bother, I just keep on goin."

"You sit, you rest, "Angel offered, "None come here but us."

The man relaxed and sat down. Angel listened for more sounds in the forest. All he heard were rabbits and birds, and a wolf passing by.

"Where you go? "Angel asked.

"I don't know. "He answered, "Maybe I can find a place where I won't be treated like a slave."

"Maybe you go to town and work." Angel offered.

"That'd be the first place massa Josiah be lookin for me, "He said, "He probly there now. He be thinkin I'd be goin where I can find food."

"Why he want you, if you run away?" Angel asked.

The man smiled, and said, "You are a indian, you probly don't know nothin bout this. Massa Josiah, he bought me at the auction. I is worth maybe 15 dollars ifn he can find a farmer out in the settlement out to the west."

Angel was puzzled. He had known of slaves, captured by other tribes. He wondered if this man had done anything wrong, but, he did not act like he had been bad, and if he had only been a captured slave, there was no reason to fear him.

"We have much deer to eat, Angel said, "you eat here."

Angel wondered about this slave. Most slaves were good sized, strong men. The smaller men were usually left to die, or killed on the spot, this man was not any taller than Angel, and, Angel was still growing.

Angel heard the call from the trees.

"We hide." He told the slave, "Men come."

He showed the slave a hiding place where he would be safe, and found his own spot to watch what would happen.

Three men came out of the forest, with rifles, following the prints the slave left. They stopped and looked around. They even looked in the trees.

"The tracks stop here." One said.

"Don't see nobody though." Another added.

The third man nodded, "Been somebody here though, they's a camp fire, and a hut. Looks like a injun camp. But only a couple a injuns."

"Well, look around see if we can find a trail, he had ta go somewhere." the second man replied.

"I don't understand Jeb," The first voice complained, "We's spendin all this time chasin that little negro, and he ain't hardly worth the time, ain't gonna bring hardly any money, and he keeps getting away. He definitely ain't worth the time or trouble he's causin."

Jeb replied, "We're bein paid to follow orders. Orders is to find the negro and bring him back."

Angel heard another sound from behind the searchers. More men were closing in on the camp.

The searchers heard it too.

"Think maybe that's the boy? The third man said.

Before anyone could answer an arrow whizzed through the air, and the first man fell to the ground. One of the men drew his rifle, but not in time. Another arrow pierced his side. Jeb took off running through the forest, as the braves came into view. They looked over their kill and made sure they were dead.

Then went after Jeb.

Two more braves appeared from the forest. One looked around and said.

"This is the work of Avenging Spirit," and he yelled, "Come out Avenging Spirit!"

Angel climbed down from the tree he was hiding in, and greeted the brave.

"I am honored to have Bear Claw in my camp." He said.

Bear Claw motioned to the other brave and the brave began dragging the lifeless bodies out of the camp.

"This is where you make your camp?" Bear Claw asked.

"It has been a good place to stay, close to the water, but not too close to the pale skins town." He answered. "it has served me well."

"Yes, it is hidden from view," Bear Claw noted, "But, now it will be known. The trail these pale skins make is easy to follow."

Angel looked at the tracks that now traveled through the camp, shook his head, and muttered.

"Yes, it looks like it won't be hidden any more."

Bear Claw was looking too, and commented.

"I see you are not alone, is Wild Flower near by?"

Wild Flower came out and nodded.

"I am with my brave," She admitted, "I am to be his squaw."

Bear Claw nodded.

"You will do well together. Who is this other?"

Angel nodded, and said.

"The one the pale skins were chasing. He is a darker skin than we are. We gave him refuge."

You are not afraid he may be a danger?" Bear Claw asked.

Angel replied, "He has not acted like an enemy. He is trying to escape the pale skins. I feel he will bring no harm."

The brave returned to the camp, and nodded at Bear Claw.

"Be very careful Avenging Spirit, we do not know of these people, they do not have the same code of honor as our people. Until our paths cross again, I wish you good hunting, and a prosperous life."

Angel nodded and replied.

"May the spirits be with you Bear Claw."

With that the two braves followed the trail Jeb and the other braves made.

Angel went to the place he hid the dark skinned man and said.

"You come out now."

The man came out.

"What people call you?" Angel asked.

"They just call me Joe." He replied.

"All people gone now, it safe to come out, they not come back." Angel stated.

The three went about stoking the fire and preparing the deer for cooking. Angel became curious and asked.

"How come you slave Joe?"

Joe, looked at Angel and smiled.

"I was born a slave." Joe answered, "My papa told me he came to this country on a ship. Said we came from a place called Congo. He said our people was invaded by a muslim group and sold to slave traders. When I turned 18 I was sold to Josiah, he gonna sell me to some farmer, or somethin and make money. I'm tired of bein a slave, I want to see what it feels like to be free."

Angel nodded, as he set the meat on the spit, over the fire. Wild Flower sat at the end of the spit, and began to turn the meat over the fire.

"You know to hunt, and fish?" Angel wondered.

"I've done my share a fishin. Joe replied, "I figure I can git by if they's a fishin hole around. I know how to hunt, but I ain't never been allowed to have a weapon to hunt with. They's afraid to give a slave a knife, he might want to use it on the massa."

Angel thought for a moment, and wondered.

"soon cold come, maybe you should go toward the warm places. If not in house, could die from cold."

Joe considered that idea, and commented.

"I guess I should think about that sort of thing, but, I can't let no white man see me til I can get the respect of a free man. I seed how people act around the white folks, with them "Yes sirs, and yes ma'ams", and I seed the way they acts around us colored folk, callin names and such. Then I seed this Josiah, he a free man. And the whites treats him bad too. "He spouted," My father said that he been treated better here than in the Congo. He said, at least the massa feeds him twice a day. I'm thinkin I can feed myself twice a day. And if'n I can't, maybe I don't need to be takin up space anyway."

"You say that being slave better than living at Congo?" Angel asked.

"My father said sometimes in the Congo the whole tribe misses meals for whole days at a time. You not only gotta watch for the animals that'll eat ya, but, other families'll kill ya too, just cause you ain't their family. Said he went hungry a lot back there. Said he didn't much like comin over here, but, sure was happy to get fed every day." Joe related, "Seems like livin on your own ain't so easy if you is in the wrong neighborhood. But I wanna try it out. Maybe I'll go back to bein a slave if things don't work out, but I gotta try."

Angel understood some of what Joe said, he knew of renegade tribes that would kill other tribes because they were other tribes, and some renegades that were of the same family but didn't like the chiefs in their tribe. They would still kill their own family members if the need came about.

Joe began again.

"I was listenin to a white man talk about people once. He said that all people came from just two people once. He was talkin about that black, white, red, and yellow people had the same parents once.

That would mean we all fight our own family when we fight each other. Don't know that it's true, but he sounded like he knew what he was sayin."

Wild Flower broke up the conversation.

"Food ready, we eat now." She said.

Angel's surprise was obvious, he said.

"You talk pale skin talk!"

"I said, if you learn pale skins words, I learn pale skins words" she giggled.

They all took of the deer meat and ate.

Chapter
TWENTY

The morning was bright and warm as Angel brought Wild Flower into the town for her first meeting with the pale skins. He was not use to entering the east gate, but decided it would be better if they did not go by Heidi's house. The house Angel had been given was on the eastern side of the camp anyway, why cause more trouble than necessary. Joe decided to stay at their camp for a few days. He felt comfortable there for now, and would move on when he felt things had died down.

Wild Flower felt the stares as she walked through this strange place. The idea of permanent housing was foreign to her. The idea of a fire inside a house didn't seem right. She noticed the odd tools, the wagons made to be drawn by horses, in fact, the horses were new to her. This would be only the second time she had seen a horse. The clothing was different, the hats confused her. This was a whole new world.

Looking into this "house" was a new thing too. It was darker than the huts she was use to.

The aroma was wooden, but, not as the natural trees. It was stuffy. And dry. She looked at the fire pit. It was made of stone, and had a place for a stack of wood. There was a wall, with a door off to one side of the house. She watched as Angel opened the door, and there was another house in the door. It was much smaller, and had a strange wooden frame with some type of fabric on top of it.

She wasn't sure why Angel laid down on it and acted like he might fall asleep.

Angel had taken a torch and set fires in small things that lit up the house. She was happy about that because the sunlight only came through the square holes the builders had left in the house. She began to understand why the house smelled the way it did. Those light makers smelled odd. There was another structure in the small house with some sort of tiers on it. When Angel pulled on one it opened up and there was a storage place there. He showed that each of those tiers had another storage place.

"This house is too big, Little Bear." She said, as she looked at the covering on top of the walls.

Angel smiled, "I remember, once, you said you did not like the squaws fighting over who got to be at just the right part of the fire pit. You said it was wrong that you only had a small place to sleep. You said it would be good to have a place to put things so you would know where to look for them. "He paused and continued, "Now, I have given you what you said you wanted, and you tell me you don't want, what you said you I wanted."

Wild Flower sneered at Angel, and grumbled.

"Sometimes Little Bear is too smart." And she pounced on Angel and wrestled him to the floor. She paused, noticing that the floor was made of wood, not ground. That pause allowed Angel to roll her over so he was on top. He looked down into her eyes and whispered.

"Smart enough to beat Wild Flower."

Wild flower began wriggling and jerking around to overthrow Angel, and he began to laugh.

Wild Flower stopped and look up at Angel. He bent down to kiss her, and she bucked him off. The match continued for several minutes until Wild Flower finally got on top.

"Now, wise one, "She said, as she bent down toward Angel's face, "I am the one who will tell you what to remember." She bent down and kissed Angel, and held him down, and he didn't seem to mind.

Wild Flower laid out on top of Angel and said.

"I do not mind this kissing."

Angel countered, "We have no chief, or tribe to announce our coming together, how can we come together without the ceremony?"

"What ceremony did you have with Heidi?" Wild Flower fired back.

It was getting dark when Wild Flower went to fetch the water. The lake was close to their house.

She watched the new people, and how they acted, and reacted to each other. She was determined to know these people. She watched their greetings, she watched the way they walked, she listened to them talking. As she returned to the house she saw a man In the strange clothes come to the door of her house and knock. Angel opened the door and allowed the visitor in. The door opened as she arrived, and Angel was walking out with the visitor.

"I must see the colonel," He said as he held the door for Wild Flower. "I will not be too long, "He promised.

"Angel," the colonel began, "Tomorrow we meet with chief Brown Feather. I want to be sure we are all ready for that meeting."

"Yes, colonel." Angel answered, "I ready."

"Is there anything we should take with us, or we should know about Brown Feather before we go?"

Angel shook his head, "This just meeting, no need to do, just talk."

The colonel went over his plan and the two talked about the coming day. The colonel seemed to want to make a big deal out of this, like a ritual ceremony, but, Angel tried to make it clear that there was no great ritual to having a meeting. They were going to get to know each other. The chief only wanted to see the face, and hear the voice of the one he was dealing with. Major Matt was there and it appeared he would be going too.

Two privates, and major Matt escorted Angel back to his house, discussing how the meeting would go. A settler, passing through the town met the group on their way.

"What did this savage do, soldiers?" He asked.

"This man, "the major stated, "is going to bring peace to us so we can live without the threat of war with those "savages", mister. Oh, and by the way," he added, "If you plan on living here, or farther west, you had better remember those "savages" out number you in this land. You might want to learn to get along with them."

"Ain't no reason for me to make friends with animals." the settler said. "I kill animals."

Angel thought of showing the man just how savage a person could be, but, the major reacted first.

"And who is the "savage "mister." He countered, "the indians want to make peace, they want to stop the killing. I suggest that you stay within the walls of a fort if you continue with that attitude."

The settler grumbled about sticking up for one's own kind and walked away. The major looked at Angel and said, "I guess some people have to learn the hard way, Angel."

Angel stuck up his fist and said, "This pale skin asks to be killed."

Angel got back to his house. The soldiers left as he opened the door. Wild Flower had seen him coming and pressed herself against him as she kissed him.

Angel explained the trip he would take in the morning. She decided she would go too. Angel protested, "This is a meeting for men, not for squaws."

"I know Brown Feather, I know many of his braves, Why can I not come with you?" Wild Flower demanded.

"This is not for games and memories, this is to stop a war!" Angel commanded, "You will stay here!"

Wild Flower saw the determination in Angel's eyes. She realized he was very serious. She pressed herself against him again and answered.

"Yes, my strong brave. I will stay."

Chapter
TWENTY ONE

Angel would rather walk, but, the colonel wanted to ride, so Angel would get to ride a horse for the second time. It seemed a bit much to bring along a platoon of soldiers when only three would actually be present at the meeting, but Angel had learned the pale skins had some weird habits. And he knew Brown Feather would have some braves in the forest to cover his back too.

When they reached the clearing the sergeant spread the platoon out in the forest to cover the area. The Colonel, Major Matt, and Angel would go into the clearing alone. Brown Feather was waiting. Angel scanned the area before he dismounted. He saw three braves in the forest, and one with Brown feather. He thought there were at least two more hidden somewhere. There did not appear to be too much trust on either side of this meeting.

"Brown Feather," Angel began the introductions, "This is Major Matt, and the Colonel.

"Colonel, Major Matt, this is Brown Feather."

The Colonel extended his hand, Brown Feather nodded and waved his hand at the tree stumps for them to sit. Angel saw the confusion and offered.

"Colonel, Brown Feather ready to talk, sit,"

The Colonel began and Angel started to interpret.

"The Colonel says he wants to have peace between his people and ours."

And Brown Feather replied, and Angel realized he was in the middle.

"Brown Feather say, pale skins come to our land and destroy land and people as they go. If pale skins want peace, must first become peaceful."

"Colonel says, most of our people are peaceful, there are always some who cause trouble, even in your tribes, some want to cause trouble. We must first admit that there will be those who will cause trouble."

Brown Feather nodded.

"Brown Feather say," Angel interpreted, "Will agree some cause trouble, both tribes"

"The Colonel says, some troubles will be small enough that we should let their own people decide how to punish them."

"Brown Feather, say, Pale skins stay on own land, pale skins punish, pale skins on Cherokee land, Cherokee punish."

"The colonel says, If one of our people gets lost and wanders onto your land, will you punish them, and not show compassion?"

"Brown Feather say, If pale skin lost, will not cause trouble, will help. If pale skins hunt only from town to the going down of the sun, to great waterfall, should not get lost."

"The Colonel says, If all goes well, Brown Feather, we may be able to share some of our things with you and you with us. We have tools and things your people can use to make life easier, and you have blankets and knowledge of the land that we can use to help our people."

Brown Feather's eyes squinted as he talked to Angel.

"Brown Feather say, my people have made agreements with pale skins before, and pale skins not honor promise. They say go beyond mountains, pale skins not bother. Now, pale skins say let us bother and you be safe. How do I believe pale skins will honor agreement?"

The Colonel fidgeted for a moment, and answered.

"The colonel says, I did not make the promise you speak of. And I can only promise what I can control. I control what happens among my people, in my town. And I do not have as much control as even I would like. But, I will promise that as long as I have that control, I will keep my promises."

Brown Feather saw the futility of the colonel's statement, and realized this would not be a truly amicable arrangement, but he decided to get to know this pale skin to test his honor. The three talked back and forth for hours getting to know each other. Sharing stories and sizing each other up. By the time the sun was past it's highest point they had agreed to at least a temporary peace agreement that both could live with. When the colonel and the major rose to go to their horses Brown Feather motioned to Angel.

"This man will honor his words. But even he says he may leave and another replace him who may not keep these words. Avenging Spirit, you can watch them from inside. Be very careful, and learn for us what to do."

Angel understood the command and replied, "I will watch Brown Feather, I will see. If I see danger I will tell you."

Brown Feather rose and turned and walked away. Angel went to his horse and rode back with the pale skins.

The colonel was happy. He had managed his first treaty with an indian. He thought he got a pretty good deal being allowed to control the wagon trains route, in and out of town, getting some good hunting ground on the west side of town. He looked over at Angel and said.

"Hey, thanks a lot Angel for being a good scout. You have been helping our town since the day we arrived. I am in your debt, the town owes you, and I don't know how we'll pay you back."

Angel smiled.

"Colonel, I don't like to see fight. I don't want people hurt, I try to make peace with all men. Not all men want to make peace."

The drums began to sound as the group was nearing the east gate.

The Colonel looked at Angel.

"What is that all about? He asked.

"Brown Feather call for counsel, to speak to other tribes. Cannot know of rules until told." Angel replied. "I will go to this counsel. I will take Wild Flower."

The colonel smiled," that sounds like an excellent idea. You deserve a break for your efforts."

As they came into view of Angel's house, he saw Wild Flower hauling water from the lake.

There was a yell. A man started moving in her direction, yelling as he picked up speed.

Angel couldn't understand his words, but the Major did, and he kicked his horse into a gallop and jumped on the man before he got too close to Wild Flower.

"Why you defending that savage?" the man was saying as he fought with the major. The colonel had already ordered some privates to take the man into custody.

"You will not attack any citizen in this town mister!" The major threatened, "Especially the squaw of our best scout!"

"But, she's a redskin, she's trouble, she'll kill all of us if you let her go." The man that Angel recognized as the settler that had confronted him before was saying.

The soldiers took the man away to the stockade.

"He'll be leaving in the morning." The major said, "Just needs a night to think things over."

Angel ran to Wild Flower and held her. Wild Flower was shaken, but didn't understand why the man was running toward her. As they got to the house, Angel looked around to the major and nodded his thanks. The major said.

"You saved my wife and son, I saved your squaw, and I still owe you."

Angel nodded and smiled as he closed the door.

The drums became louder, and other drums replied to the first drums. The town began to get nervous, but the colonel sent the soldiers out to calm everyone down. Wild Flower brightened looking at Angel and asked.

"We go to counsel Little Bear? Squaw can go to counsel."

Angel smiled and answered, "Squaw can go to counsel. Whole Cherokee tribe will see Little Bear and Wild Flower together."

Wild Flower hugged Angel, and kissed him, and added, "Yes, Wild Flower does like kisses."

Chapter
TWENTY TWO

It was well after dark before the drums stopped beating. There had been at least eight drums answering the call. The drums would begin again in the morning, until all were gathered. Many would come to a counsel that is so soon after the normal counsel. It had to be serious.

Angel spent that night with wild Flower in town. They would have plenty of time to get there tomorrow. The bed was much softer than the ground. And the rain had started falling shortly after the sun was gone. They would stay dry, and be out of any wind that might come up.

The drums began again as Angel and Wild Flower began their trip to the counsel. The ground was still wet, but the storm had passed. When they got to Brown Feather's camp Wild Flower went to see some of her old friends and announce that she had become a squaw. Angel decided he would meditate in the forest before facing the counsel. He knew he would be the center of attention, he was the main link in this situation. He needed some time to relax and think. He pondered how likely it would be that this agreement would last for very long. He had seen the bigotry on both populations. He knew that most of the people, on both sides, were of a peaceful spirit, but, there were also many, on both sides that would hate because of their differences.

"The question, "The brave said, "is which side will you take when the war begins."

Angel whirled around to see the brave sitting on a tree stump. His hand was on his knife by the time he realized he had met this brave before. Angel had a weird feeling come over him this time. Every time he met this brave something had happened, or was about to happen. The brave waved Angel to sit on a stump near to his. As Angel sat, the brave began to speak.

"One of the worst and most damaging hatreds is the hatred of skins." He said, "you have seen three skins, and every one is afraid of the other two skins. The pale skins are afraid because they know they are taking Cherokee land, and they would kill over land that is their's. The dark skins because most are owned by other men, who treat them as animals. And the Cherokee because their land is being destroyed by the invasion of the pale skins."

"But which one is right?" Angel asked.

"They are all right." The brave acknowledged, "It is right that you should not give up your land, it is right that men should not be slaves, it is right that the pale skins need new places to live. And it is right that all three should fight to do what they know is right."

Angel blinked and asked, "Which one will win."

"The one that fights the best will win." The brave replied, "Think of what you have seen so far Avenging Spirit. You have seen the soldiers kill your people, you have seen your people make the pale skins ask for peace. And you have seen a slave that found his freedom, at least for now. There have been victories for all three, and there will be more from all three. But, what will make the difference will be which one has the best weapons, and the best shooters."

"Then," Angel muttered, "The pale skins will win."

The brave nodded, and added, "They bring with them those who have learned to fight as their work.

Your people only have braves who know hunting and only fight other braves. But, if they do not fight they will lose their hunting grounds, and the land that they are a part of. If they do fight they must face the pale skin's rifles."

"So, what do I tell the counsel?" Angel speculated.

The brave shook his head and said, "It will not matter what you say. There will be many who will hear you and want to live peacefully, and those who will not hear you, but, only try to make war. Some will show you great honor, and some will feel betrayed by you. You must do what you feel is right." And with that the brave rose and left Angel to think on what he had learned.

The drums ceased, as Angel rose to go back to the counsel. He felt more confused than when he walked into the forest. He came by Wild Flower and her friends, who giggled as he walked by. He was much too deep in thought to pay attention to them. When he got to the fire pit he sat with the braves and listened to them talk.

"They have offered us peace if we leave them on our land."

"But it is our land. How can we let them take our land?"

"It is better to share our land than to be killed on our land."

"It is better to die on our land than to let the pale skins destroy our land."

The arguments lasted through the day, and well into the night. Finally, they all went to their tents for the night. Wild Flower asked what was happening, and Angel said, "So far mostly just talk, tomorrow would bring the decisions of what we will do."

"All of the tribes know that we are together now Little Bear." Wild Flower boasted.

"Then why are you so far away squaw." Angel growled.

Wild Flower laughed, and closed in on her brave. "We are not so far apart now Little Bear." She cooed.

The morning brought on more talk, and arguing. Voices got loud, voices got soft, this matter was more than just disagreements, there were threats and physical attacks that had to be broken up.

Angel watched quietly, and he noticed Brown Feather was silent too. But, after several hours of listening to all that was being said, Brown Feather stood up and waved the meeting into silence.

"I have talked to the leader of the pale skins," He began, "He said he wants peace. I believe he is an honorable man. I also know that not all pale skins are honorable. I have agreed to try to make peace in our land, and the pale skins have agreed too. "Brown Feather looked around the group, and continued.

"You have all been told what our agreement is. I hear the calls for peace, I hear the demands for war.

But, from the one who has been in both camps I have heard nothing. Avenging Spirit, I would hear what you think, you too have heard the braves here talk of their desire for peace, or war. Speak to us of what you know." Brown Feather sat down, And Angel rose and began to speak.

"My brothers, I have heard your words. There is much to disagree about, but this is mostly a question of who this land belongs to." Angel paused, and looked at his audience, "My father told me a long time ago, that our ancestors came into this land to make it their own. They fought the animals, and many died. Many died from the herbs that fought against our people, until we learned the ones we should leave alone. The rain fought our people, as did the cold. But we took this land to ourselves. He told me that one of the beliefs our people always agreed on was that the land does not belong to any of us. We are only caretakers, and we must leave the land to our heirs."

"These pale skins are much the same as our ancestors. Some have already died from the animals of this land, some have eaten the bad herbs, they have fought the rain, and will learn of the cold that will come. They also fought our people, some because they do not like the difference in our skin, and some because we fought back. I too have killed five pale skins that killed my family."

There was an approving moan from the audience. Angel continued.

"They have offered a chance to have peace, even when we all know there are those in any tribe that will kill even their own people. I have heard from those who feel that the only way to peace is to kill the pale skins, but they have better weapons than we have, and there are more of them coming. My feeling is that if we have peace, even if only for a time, we can learn of their weapons. We can learn how they fight." Angel paused again scanned the counsel.

"Our father's taught us to hunt." He said, "Before we reached the age to become braves we had already learned the habits of our prey. We had learned of how to trap them, and catch them. This is why we have survived. This prey we do not know yet. We have not learned of their habits, we do not know how to trap them, or catch them. We should take the time to learn these things. And this peace they offer will give us that time. Once we know how to fight them, and maybe learn how to use their weapons, we will have a much better chance to win."

The crowd stayed silent contemplating all they had heard. Chief Red Eagle was the first to rise.

"Avenging Spirit is wise for being so young, "He said, "Your father taught you well. If we can learn of these pale skins we will know better how to fight them. I can agree with this plan."

"But we cannot trust that the pale skins will honor this pledge." Running Deer exclaimed.

"We cannot trust that you will honor this pledge Running Deer." Brown Feather replied. "But, Avenging Spirit is right. We need to find the ways to overcome this people or we will die. My tribe killed many pale skins, so many their chief came to me to make peace. He told me that if there is no peace he will have to kill us all. And I believe they can do that with their rifles. They will not spare the old or the young if this happens."

The arguments continued for a while, but, finally, it was agreed that it would be best to take some time to decide what to do. As the counsel began to disperse Angel went toward his tent. The women understood that a decision had been made, and went to their tents to know what had happened.

As Wild Flower approached her brave she smiled and offered.

"We heard you speak Little Bear, you spoke well."

Angel smiled, "The spirits have been good to me Wild Flower." He said.

Red Eagle came to Angel and said, "Buffalo Hunter would be proud to see his son this day, Avenging Spirit. You have become a great leader of your people."

Angel's face flushed, he stammered a little and replied, "I am honored, Chief Red Eagle, that you feel this way."

The chief turned and went to his tribe. Angel and Wild Flower took down their tent, and started the trek back to the town.

Chapter
TWENTY THREE

The days turned into weeks. There was calm. Wagon trains had come and gone. Angel had watched and learned how to clean, load, and fire a rifle, and a pistol. He had watched how the soldiers guarded the town. He had inspected the wall around the town. He found parts that were not as stable as most of the wall was. He felt he was treated well by the town's people, but, he also knew where not to go, for there were those that would do him harm.

Wild Flower met many women and had learned some of their words. She knew how to greet them and was learning to talk with them. She knew how fragile they were compared to indian women.

She tried to avoid Heidi when she could, but there did not seem to be any anger between the two. Heidi seemed happy to forget Angel, but she did seem to be gaining weight. Wild Flower worried about that.

Angel and Wild Flower had made a trip to the hut where they met Joe. He had not been there for some time. He had taken one rifle with him, and left one behind. There was still a powder horn, and bullets too. Wild Flower watched as Angel cleaned the barrel and hid the weapon out of sight.

"Do you think there will be war, Little Bear?" she wondered.

Angel stared at the weapon and said, "It will come Wild Flower. You have heard the signals from the tribes. One killed to the east, one to the north, and our people have killed more than a few pale skins. It will come."

As they approached the east gate Angel noticed the wind had changed. He thought for a moment and said, "The wind is from the north, it will be cooler tonight." Even as he spoke the rain drops began to fall. They hurried to their house. Before the rain became a deluge.

The sky had become dark with clouds. The rain came pouring down, and the wind began to blow. This would be a violent storm. The sky would light up, and then return to darkness. The thunder was becoming louder. Wild Flower held on to Angel and wondered, "The spirits must be very angry tonight, Little Bear, I am afraid."

Angel looked out at the sky through the hole in the wall, and answered, "Perhaps at others, we have done nothing to upset the spirits."

Wild Flower squeezed a little tighter, "I have seen the spirits do harm to those around the place where the spirits take their revenge."

The bolt hit a wagon not 100 yards from the window Angel was looking out of. The thunder shook the house. A fire began to devour the wagon, but the amount of rain doused it quickly. Wild Flower had a strangle hold on Angel's torso. This would be a long night Angel thought, as he relished the feeling of his squaw wrapped so tightly around him.

Angel surveyed the damage from last night's storm. The broken wagon, the debris all over the road. He noticed parts of the wall were broken. But all of the houses had withstood the storm, and none of the people were harmed. He wondered what the effects that storm had on the tribes. He decided to go and see for himself. Wild Flower would go. She was worried about her friends too.

They used the wagon's trail, which was muddy, but not cluttered with debris like the forest trails were. They heard the horses, and saw the newly made trail into the forest. The smell of the camp fires from the tribe was in the air. They ran after the horses.

The soldiers were dismounting and lashing the horses to the trees. There was one soldier left to watch the horses. They heard a sergeant saying, "don't leave an injun alive." The anger in Angel sparked an adrenaline rush. Creeping up on the guard of the horses was quick and easy. The man was not paying any attention to anything but his sore butt. Angel was able to kill the man in seconds, and with no noise. He took the man's rifle, and his powder horn, and bullets, and a sword. He and Wild Flower had followed the trail of the soldiers. They had counted ten horses, that left nine soldiers.

The soldiers had begun to spread out to encompass that side of the camp. Angel crept up on the closest soldier, who was concentrating on positioning himself to attack. He had turned around in time to feel the sword pierce his chest, but he managed a groan that would alert the other soldiers.

As Angel saw another soldier turn to see what happened. Angel swung the rifle he had down and aimed as the soldier began to draw his rifle. Angel fired first. He heard another shot ring out and turned to see wild Flower with the rifle of the soldier he had just killed, and another soldier falling from her bullet.

Wild Flower had learned a lot too. That left six. But, the tribe was warned now.

Both Angel and Wild Flower slipped back into the forest and reloaded their rifles, while other soldiers came to see what had happened. One of the soldiers came in their direction. Another easy target Angel thought. And he waited for the soldier to get close enough. Wild Flower made a noise.

The soldier swung toward her. Angel jumped at the man and stabbed him. And Wild Flower rose up and shot another soldier. Angel began to aim at another soldier when he saw braves attacking the residue of soldiers. He and Wild Flower gathered all of the powder horns and bullets and brought them into camp.

Brown Feather welcomed Angel and showed his gratitude for his help, but noted that they had heard the horses coming, and had prepared. Angel looked around the camp. It was as if there had been no storm at all in this camp. But he turned his attention back to Brown Feather.

"These soldiers were not from the town." He noted.

"No, "Bear Claw confirmed, "these are from the wagon train that is coming. We have been watching it since yesterday. There are many soldiers, and wagons."

"These soldiers came to kill." Angel acknowledged. "They intended to kill your tribe."

"A survivor from the hills told us of how they had killed all of his tribe and others before them. This wagon train brings death." Bear Claw stated. "We can no longer keep our agreement. We must survive."

Angel nodded, "This now is war!"

The drums again began to sound. This time they were drums of war. This time there would be no talk of peace.

Angel taught the braves how to load and shoot the rifles. The horses were brought in so they would have riders. Three braves were sent out to track the wagon train's approach, and cause as much trouble as they could. Angel went back to the town. This would be hard for Angel. He had made many friends in town, and now he would have to help in destroying them. The pale skins had left the tribes no choice. He had done all he could to help both sides get along together, but, now, he had to take sides, and his people were the ones that were under attack.

There were two riders coming from the east. Angel knew they were scouts for the wagon train.

They would be bringing word of the approach to the town. He would not let them get through. He did not want the town to know what was happening yet. He found a tree and climbed out on the branch.

As they drew close enough Angel threw his knife at one, and dropped down on the other. He crossed his forearm around the man's neck as they fell to the ground. The fall, and the pressure Angel applied crushed the man's wind pipe, and the other scout had fallen on the knife. Angel thought, "the spirits are with me."

It suddenly occurred to Angel that it would be much better to get rid of the approaching force than to attempt anything in town right now. He cornered the horses and headed back toward the train.

When he got to the trail the soldiers that tried to attack the tribe had made, he sent the extra horse in that direction and continued toward the train. By the time he reached the place where he could see the train, the sun was going down in the west. It would only be an hour or two before it would be dark.

He hid the horse in the forest, he would get closer on foot.

He counted thirty wagons, and could not get an accurate count of the soldiers, or the civilians that were on this train. But there were many horses. He found one of the wagons with gun powder kegs in it, and he saw what appeared to be a giant rifle on two wheels. A man came out of the camp heading toward Angel. Angel watched as he came nearer. Angel realized the man was about to relieve himself.

He considered killing the man right then, but decided not to take the chance of alerting the camp that he was there. The spirits were still with Angel, the man had disturbed a mother bear and she attacked the man he tried to run but the bear was fast. He did make it back to the camp, limping and bleeding profusely. There were three shots taken at the bear but she escaped back to her cubs. The man may have escaped the bear, but he would not be fighting for some time.

Angel heard the call of a brave, and the answer from another, he knew he had to let them know he was there too, so he called back. The soldiers were looking around. They had lowered their rifles not knowing what the calls meant, but obviously aware they were not sounds they were use to hearing.

The call came again. Angel had been moving closer to the call, and the call seemed to be moving toward him. He watched the guards looking into the darkness, and answered. Angel heard the approaching foot steps, he would make sure it was a brave before uncovering himself. When they met Angel motioned to go back into the forest where they would be less likely to be heard.

"How many braves are here?" Angel asked.

"There will be fifty by morning, Avenging Spirit." The brave answered.

"No, how many are here now!" Angel demanded.

"there are twenty braves in our camp." The brave answered.

Angel sat and thought for a few minutes and said.

"We must keep this train here, it cannot reach the town or they will have to much cover. We need to block the trail, tonight. Take ten braves and some horses and drag logs and bushes into the trail. I will see if I can cause some damage tonight."

The brave nodded and ran toward the tribe. Angel went back to his perch to watch how they were guarding their goods. There was a guard walking around the big rifle, and he turned and walked away, he was gone from site for several minutes, and made the same trip around the rifle. There was another guard walking around the powder wagon, he took even longer to go around. Angel looked to the other side of the big rifle. The same pattern around another wagon. There were five fires still burning in the camp. Angel took notice of where they were, and the best way to get to one. He didn't know what to do yet, but, He had to do something. This wasn't like the five that he had blown up to free Wild Flower. There were too many to hurt them all. But he might be able to reduce the odds. He saw that many of the men were sleeping outside of the wagons. And, the powder wagon was on a hill.

He crept as close as he dared waiting for the guard of the rifle to pass. When the guard turned to walk away Angel ran to the rifle and slid underneath it, in time to not be seen by the other two guards.

He took a position to surprise the guard that would be coming back. He launch himself at the guard and threw his forearm around his neck, and stabbed him in his neck. Then he pushed him under the rifle, and moved to the powder wagon. The guard was just getting to the rear of the wagon. Angel repeated his moves. He had to wait for the last guard's return, and, he repeated his actions for the third time. He dragged the bodies around to the powder wagon. He waited to see if there was a reaction, but no one seemed to notice.

The next step was getting a powder keg. Once he had loosened the ropes holding the kegs in place, he took one out he set the keg so he could easily open the plug in the keg. He took the rope that had been holding the kegs to the front of the wagon. He would have to be very careful now, he would be in full view of the camp for the next step. He stealthily crept to the end of the whiffle tree, (The beam the horses were yoked to) tied the rope around it and crept back, he took the other end of the rope and wrapped it around the carriage and pulled it tight. Then he took off the brake, went to the back, unplugged the keg, made sure it would spill it's contents, and then pushed as hard as he could.

The wagon began to move. Angel kept pushing as the wagon picked up speed. Angel let it go and ran as fast as he could back to the forest. The wagon kept picking up speed as it neared the fire. It ran over a soldier in it's way and yelling began. The bump of hitting the soldier turned the wagon to miss the fire, but, a keg bounced out and rolled into the fire. The explosion sent fire everywhere, including to the line the open powder keg was making. The fire followed the wagon, and came back to it's starting place.

Angel watched the camp turn to fire and when the fire finally caught up to the wagon the explosion was massive. Sparks from the explosion set off another wagon. Angel had done some damage.

At least four soldiers lay dead. Many of the horses had been scared away. These men would not see much sleep, if any, this night. Angel slipped around to the trail that was being blocked. He called to the braves, they called back. He came to see how they had done. It would not take too long to clear what hey had managed to spread across the trail, but it would hold them up for a time. Seven horses had made their way to the trail where the tribe was working. They would help make things a little harder on the train.

Angel was tired. He knew he needed to sleep to be ready for tomorrow. The battle would begin tomorrow. He tried to head back to the tribal camp but knew it would be too far. The horse he was riding stopped.

"You have had a long day Little Bear." Wild Flower said, "We will camp here."

She helped him off his horse and down to the ground.

"Why are you here!" Angel demanded, "the squaws are suppose to wait at the camp."

Wild Flower threw her hands on her hips, and claimed, "I always beat you in our fights. Why should I be left out of this one."

Angel was too tired to argue, he snuggled into his squaw's lap and fell asleep.

Chapter
TWENTY FOUR

It was the sound of passing deer that woke Angel, just before sunrise. As he rose to stretch out, Wild Flower yawned and rose from the ground.

"I like pale skin beds." She grumbled.

Angel laughed, and gave her a nudge. She tried to look angry, and reached out to slap him, Angel ducked, and tickled Wild Flower. She jumped away from Angel long enough to compose herself and lunged at her brave. Angel side-stepped his squaw, but grabbed her waist, pulled her around in front of him, as she thrashed in his arms, and he kissed her. Her arms circled his neck, and she forgot about being angry.

"We should attack the pale skins now." one brave voted, "They are weak, they will be scared." "The work of last night will be lost if we don't attack now." Another chimed in.

Angel raised his hands. "The pale skins teach," He began, "to always find the "advantage", the thing that will give you a better chance to win. This wagon train is sitting still. The defenders of it have many ways to protect themselves from our attack. If we are attacking we will be moving and not aim as well. The advantage is theirs. BUT, if we let the train go on to the place where we blocked the trail,, they will be more in the open, and we will have the trees for protection, the advantage will be ours. And by the time they get to the blocked place, all of the wagons will be in line so they cannot change their position. And we will be prepared to attack from all sides at once, and none will get away. This is the plan I offer. We will surprise them, they will not be prepared. We have the advantage."

Bear Claw stood, and commanded, "Braves,,,, I have heard the voice of the spirits in these words. I wish to win this battle. I will follow chief Avenging Spirit into battle." The braves all nodded, none could argue with this strategy.

Angel was overwhelmed by the honor Bear Claw had bestowed on him. He contemplated it as they rode into the area they would be defending. He was giving orders to braves much older than he was. He had them spread out along the trail, on either side. He made sure that the rifle carriers had bows and arrows too. He reminded them that they would only get one shot with each rifle, so they should aim well. He instructed the ones at the east end of the ambush to wait until all of the wagons were passed them, so none could turn around. Get the last wagon first. And no rider should be allowed to get away. Even one survivor could bring more soldiers too quickly.

A brave came running from the pale skin camp.

"They have broken camp," He panted, "They will be here soon."

Angel nodded, and asked, "how many wagons, and men did you see?"

"There are twenty three wagons, I could not count the men, but I counted twenty six graves." the brave answered.

"Now,,, we wait." Angel said.

Slowly the wagons came into view. It seemed to take so long to get to the point Angel wanted it to be. Suddenly, shots from the back of the wagons, and within seconds the forest was filled with smoke from gun powder. Soldiers fell like leaves from the trees. In a matter of minutes the battle was over. Shouts of victory filled the air, and braves went through the wagons and area to make sure it was finished. Then they came to where Angel was. They began to dance and yell.

Angel held up his hands until the braves quieted. He looked around and said, "This battle is over my brothers, but, the work is not done. We have wagons of rifles, and powder to move out of this place. And we must clear this trail. No one must know of this, for as long as possible." The braves went about clearing the trail, and others started to figure out how to drive the wagons. Angel made sure the wagons with the powder would be driven by braves who would be careful. He told them of the danger the powder could bring. And that if they got it into a safe place they would have a better force to fight off the pale skins. The clearing of the trail took some time, after all, they took a long time setting it up. Angel was satisfied that this trail was clear and there would be no sign of the battle that took place there.

The celebration that night was magnificent. The braves tried to dance off the adrenaline from the fight. After the chiefs allowed the braves their time to celebrate, Bear Claw stepped up and raised his hands. His look was serious.

"Now,, braves,, we have proven we can fight these pale skins." He announced, "Our warrior chief Avenging Spirit will lead us to rid our land of the pale skins." A roar went up from the crowd. "Next we will take their town!" He yelled.

Angel rose up to speak. There were cheers and laughter as he raised his hands, "Today we had a great victory over a people that came to kill us." Angel began, "There is a great difference between killing those who would kill you,, and killing those who do not want to kill. There are many women and children in the town. And many who do like us. How do we kill those who have helped us?"

"if we leave them there, more will keep coming, "Came a shout from the braves. Angel replied, "They will keep coming if the town is there or is not there. And we risk more wagon trains like this one, who will be more prepared to fight us."

Then a chief spoke up, "Avenging Spirit,, do you believe that no one will notice this wagon train disappeared?"

"No, I know it will be noticed, but not for some time." Angel speculated, "That will mean the next train will be stronger, and ready to fight. It will mean we will have to have braves out along the trail to send signals to know if a train is coming, and if it is a fighting force or just settlers. It means from this day, we cannot allow any pale skins to know where we are. It means our lives have changed, and we must either change with the land or die. Brothers! We had a great victory today. We defeated an army that we should not have defeated. We surprised them. This will not happen again. The next time they will be waiting for our surprise. Another thing the pale skins teach is that you should not make the same mistake twice. The grass and land around the place their camp blew up will be known. They will know where to start looking for trouble.

The war has begun, but, this is not a war against the helpless and the women, it is against the soldiers who would kill our people. No one at the town has done anything,,, yet,, to break their promise of peace. I am not ready to lead a battle against them, at least not now."

There was much talk among the braves. Many felt let down. They felt they had the ability to get rid of all signs of the pale skins. They wanted to take back their land. Red Eagle stood and quieted the crowd.

"I will trust Avenging spirit." He said, "He has proven himself to be a great warrior. He has shown much courage. For now, I see where he may learn enough to defeat the pale skins when we need to. But I will warn Avenging Spirit. The time will come when we will have to fight the pale skins,, to the death. Although there may be some that do not deserve to die. Our people do not deserve to die either."

Angel and Wild Flower were finally headed back to the town. Wild Flower wanted to play, but she could see Angel was deep in thought. This decision was weighing heavy on him. She could hold back no longer.

"Little Bear,, talk to me." She begged, "I know you need to talk,,, please tell me what you feel."

He looked at her and attempted a smile, and said.

"Wild Flower,,, I don't know what to do. I know the counsel is right. We will have to attack the town and get rid of the pale skins. I know they will come back with more men and more rifles. It will not end until many die. But, I don't want to kill people that have shown me kindness, taught me better ways to live. They trust me. They have cared for me when there was no one else there to care." He began to sob and tears began to well up in his eyes. "No matter which way I go,, I must do harm to people I have come to care for."

Wild Flower stopped and held Angel, and said.

"Yes, I have seen your heart divided between the people. I know you do care for both sides. I know I would not want to make the decision you must make. I have grown close to some of the women in the pale skin town too. But, I know you will make the right choice,, the spirits have been with you."

They walked along again. There was a noise. Someone was near. The pair looked to see what had made the noise. Joe walked out of the bushes, after he recognized Angel.

"Hello friend." He offered, "Hope you ain't headed back to that town."

"There is something wrong at the town?" Angel asked.

"Why, they been lookin for you for a couple a days now." He confided. "Seems like some hunters got kilt by some injuns over on the west side a town. They was some so mad they took a torch to yer house. I wouldn't go back there ifn I was you."

Angel stared at Joe for a minute and said, "You were there, in town."

Joe shrugged his shoulders, and giggled a little, "I snuck in to get some food that was layin out. Got to hear a lot through the windows. Things done been changin down there. They was talkin bout some general that was spose to be comin to take over the town. Said sompin bout a colonel movin to the west. Took a platoon or two with him."

Angel felt sick inside. He wondered, "Did you hear anything about Major Matt?" "Don't rightly know who that would be." He answered. "But one of the officers had a wife and kid. Saw em leavin."

Angel thanked Joe for the information and headed for his original perch. He looked over the area he had found Audrey, and Mathew's house was empty. Helga's house was vacant too. He looked to see where his house was, there was burned wood, and ashes, still smoldering. As he climbed down he looked at Wild Flower.

"It's all gone." He moaned. "We will return to the tribe."

Wild Flower felt Angel's sorrow. She watched his face as they started back toward the tribe. She saw it turn from sorrow to anger. Then Angel stopped and turned to Wild Flower, "You wait for me right here." He commanded, "I will return."

Angel ran through the trees and vanished for what seemed like a long time. When he did return He took Wild Flower's hand and started toward the tribe again.

"It will be easy now." He chirped, "The soldiers that they were expecting will never show up. They only have a few men left to guard the town." The pair hurried to the tribal camp.

Chapter
TWENTY FIVE

Angel had caused quite a stir when he came to Bear Claw and announced he was ready to rid the land of the pale skins. Many braves had gone back to their own camps. The drums would have to call again. Angel explained that the defending force had never been this low they should attack the town now. He knew the gates had towers and guards that could see any attackers from a long distance. He knew that there was an area on the east end where the wall did not go all the way to the lake. It would not be easy getting through there though because the guards could see that portion of the wall.

Angel remembered the parts of the wall that were not as well built as the others. He also knew there would be no guards in those areas. One of those places was behind the saloon. They had not used logs to build that piece of the wall. There was a five foot section that was merely slats of wood, but it was up against a stand of bushes that could create a lot of noise to penetrate. Another was near one man's house. This one would be very easy to get to and through. This man wanted a way to get out of town without using the gates. There would only be room for one brave at a time, but, it could be done quickly and easily. There was one other section that could be of use. It was near the headquarters.

There would be many soldiers in that area. It was near the barracks too. But, it was not a large section, again only one could pass through it at a time.

They had two wagons of powder, and three wagons of rifles, and bullets, that huge rifle on two wheels, knives, uniforms, pistols, two wagons with tools, and three wagons of dry goods, (There had been more wagons of dry goods, three were still well stocked).

Wild Flower came to her brave.

"It's getting late Little Bear." She stated, "I am proud of my Chief. But, it is time for rest."

Angel nodded, and added.

"I cannot attack tonight, tomorrow we can prepare." He followed his squaw to their tent. She gave him some food to eat. After he had devoured the meal, Wild Flower went to the tent and began to enter saying, "If you need someone to attack, tonight, "as she closed the flap of the tent. Angel rose and smiled, shook his head, and followed Wild Flower.

By the time the sun was high in the sky, Angel felt enough braves had come to begin to explain his plan. "We have rifles and wagons and clothing of the pale skins. They are expecting wagons to arrive soon. If we wear soldiers clothes, we will be able to ride those wagons right into the town. We can have eight braves in each wagon, and two drivers. We will use three wagons for that. There will be fifty rifles in each wagon. We will have ten riders on horses around the wagons. That will be forty braves that will enter through the east gate. We will have to look like pale skin soldiers.

Once we get inside, the first thing we must do is kill the guards at the gate. There will be four on the wooden path on top of the wall, and two at the bottom. Those should be killed by braves in the first wagon, while the third is passing through it. From that time on remember not to kill other braves.

There will be three groups that will attack from other places." Angel moved over to the map he had drawn, in the dirt, of the town. "We will need at least three braves for each of the openings that are not guarded." And he pointed out the areas they would be found. In this one closest to the west, there should be five braves, with three kegs of powder," He pointed to the drawings he had made of the buildings. "This," He said, "is the building we want to blow up. It is where the soldiers that are not guarding will be. The five will have to sneak in, with those kegs and place them along the building.

You will have to pour a line of powder back to the opening in the wall. I will give you the lights the pale skins use to light up their houses to light the powder. You should have enough time to run to a spot where you can shoot the guards on the west gate when the powder goes off. They will be looking to see what is happening. You will set up and be ready to light the powder when you hear the sounds of the rifles on the other side of the camp. We will have three braves at this spot to get behind the pale skins." He pointed to the house with the opening. He decided to forget the one with the bushes against it. "The rest can run in after the guards on the east wall are gone. The only trouble we should have are the pale skins that hide in the houses. This attack will not be as easy as the last,because we will be moving more than the pale skins, but, if we look enough like pale skins to get in, we will be able to surprise them and will have a better chance of not getting many of our braves hurt."

A voice in the crowd shouted, "ADVANTAGE!"

Angel nodded, "advantage." and smiled.

The tribe went about trying on the uniforms and deciding who would go where. Angel showed them they would have to stuff their hair inside the hats they would have to wear. They would have to have boots on. Angel put on the generals uniform. It didn't fit well but Wild Flower managed to make it look reasonably good. A little padding here, some tightening there. The horses were hitched to the wagons. They added three more wagons just for looks, and headed to the trail.

Six wagons, one huge rifle, two soldiers to the rear, two soldiers to the front, and three on either side. And Angel in front leading the train. As they came out into the open, where the guards of the town could see them, Angel looked at the guards. When they saw the approaching train they began to shout at the guards on the ground. The gates began to open. It all looked good, so far.

It seemed a long time to finally get to the gate, but Angel wanted to take his time and not upset any of the guards. The guards saluted as Angel came under the wall, Angel returned the salute. He began to count, one wagon, two wagons, another soldier saluted.

Angel returned that salute. Three wagons.

Shots rang out, and soldiers fell. Angel dismounted and began shooting his pistols until he got back to the wagon that held his bow and arrows. The multiple explosions from the west side of the town caused total chaos throughout the town. Horses began bucking and running. Angel ran beside a wagon headed toward the headquarters and found a house to give him cover. He looked back to see how it was going. He saw pale skins falling, and some braves had been hit. Braves were entering houses and killing all inside. As he looked to the other side he saw soldiers coming to enter the battle.

The powder kegs had done their job. Not many came out of the barracks. Angel got out of the uniform as he watched the battle. Once he was free of the clothes he found his way to the building that held the gun powder for the soldiers. He knew that there would be soldiers in the headquarters building that would wait to enter the fight. He had found a great fondness for the powder. Grabbing two kegs he worked his way toward the building. Going around houses. Ducking behind wagons. He made it to the headquarters. He set one keg down by the side of the building, opened the second keg and began to make a line from the first keg. He saw soldiers in his way. He sat the keg down and reached for the rifle he still carried. He aimed at one of the soldiers. The soldier went down before Angel pulled the trigger. The other soldiers turned and began to shoot in the direction of the shot. Angel picked off another of the soldiers. The last one ran toward the fight.

Angel picked up the keg again and started toward the fire of the barracks. When he made it all the way to the barracks, he finished the line and threw the keg into the fire, and ran as fast as he could to the wall. The line fired up with an explosion and traveled straight to the headquarters. The blow collapsed the building. Soldiers ran out, some on fire. Angel brought his bow from behind his back, and began shooting at the soldiers. Soon he saw the other braves making their way to the west gate.

The battle was over. The tribes had lost only ten braves. The pale skins had lost all that were in the town. Angel did not feel good about this battle. He knew it had to be, but, he was sad the town was gone. He felt like he had lost as much as he had gained.

Chapter
TWENTY SIX

Angel had taken a bed from one of the houses and put it on a wagon, with some tools and headed back to the tribal camp. There would be a great celebration this night. Angel would be honored again. But this time, he didn't feel right about it. He didn't feel like a hero, in fact, he felt a little sick inside about the whole thing. But, he would have to allow this night to be a celebration.

It was when Bear Claw stood and announced.

"As of this day, the Cherokee nation will triumph over the pale skins. We have a great leader, and warrior chief with the power of the spirits. We cannot be beaten.", Angel had to stand, and say.

"Today we have had a great victory. We killed many people. We destroyed a town. And we rid our land of a different skin color than our own. Yet, we know more will come. We know many more of our people and theirs will die. We only lost ten of our own in this battle. But there will be more. I do not want to be a part of killing more people. My father taught me to pray over each animal you must kill to eat, because you have taken a life. That did not happen today. There were no prayers for the deaths that happened today. There was joy and celebration for taking the lives of others." Angel paused, scanned the crowd and added, "I do not feel good about this victory. I feel bad for the pale skins that died just because they chose to try to live on our land. I feel bad for the Cherokee who will die because of this victory. And I feel bad for those who think we have won this war."

Angel thought to leave at that moment, but, knew he must continue.

"I will not be leading you to more victories. I have had enough killing for a lifetime. I will go into the forest and live with nature."

Angel left the celebration and went to his tent, to his squaw, He said, "come Wild Flower. It is time to find our peace together. "They walked to the wagon he had prepared for their departure. She saw he had filled it with dry goods, and tools, and rifles and powder. She smiled at Angel and said.

"My wonderful brave, you brought me a pale skin bed." and she wrapped her arms around him and kissed him.

Bear Claw came to Angel and said, "Avenging Spirit, if you will go I will go. You will make a great chief. And if we need to fight again, I want you to lead me." And he and several others followed Angel's wagon.

As they drove away Angel talked about his plans to build a pale skin house to live through the cold times, and how much better things would be with all of these new tools they could use. Wild Flower leaned against her brave and said, "Better for all three of us Little Bear."

By the next moon, the pale skins were again passing through the land that had seen so much death. A new town was built, and many Cherokee died trying to take their land back. The pale skins that came this time killed all the indians they found. Brown Feather sent a brave to find Avenging Spirit.

It took four months to finally find the meadow, in the valley where Angel's house stood. The cold had passed. The birds sang outside the house. And inside the great chief was coddling his son.

Angel said he would not go back. He would not kill again. Then the brave reminded him.

"Avenging Spirit, one day your son will want a squaw, Where will you go to find one for him?"

Angel pondered that idea for a long time.